the vampire slayer™

COLONY

Buffy the Vampire Slayer™

Available from POCKET BOOKS

STAKE YOUR DESTINY

COLONY

Laura J. Burns AND Melinda Metz

An original novel based on the hit television series created by Joss Whedon

POCKET BOOKS

LONDON • SYDNEY • NEW YORK • TORONTO

POCKET
BOOKS

POCKET BOOKS
An imprint of Simon & Schuster
Africa House, 64–78 Kingsway, London WC2B 6AH

Printed and bound in Great Britain

First Edition 10 9 8 7 6 5 4 3 2 1

A CIP catalogue number for this book is available from the British Library

ISBN: 1-4165-0238-6

STAKE YOUR DESTINY

Into every generation a chosen one is born who will stand alone against the vampires, the demons, and the forces of darkness. In this generation it's you, Buffy Summers of Sunnydale, California—high school student by day, Slayer of the undead by night. It's a tough gig, but somebody's gotta do it.

Now, this sacred birthright thing comes with a few rules: Always listen to your Watcher, never fall in love with a vampire, and, whatever you do, do not read this book in sequential order.

Okay, you can ignore those first two rules, but the last is nonnegotiable. Make sure to follow the messages at the bottom of the page—they'll let you make a choice regarding the story line, giving you a different page to turn to depending on what action you decide to take. As usual, the fate of the world is in your hands, so choose carefully. And isn't it about time you got to make your own decisions?

Break a leg—just make sure it's not your own.

Turn to page 1. . . .

Prologue

You walk into the Sunnydale High auditorium in your these-boots-are-made-for-walkin' boots. Problem is, with the extreme pointy toes, they're not so much made for walking. More like made for squeezing all your little piggies into one club of angry red flesh. Bad choice buying these babies, even though they are so, so pretty. You slide into the empty spot next to your best guy pal, Xander, and stick your feet up on the seat in front of you. Ahh, relief from the pain.

Principal Snyder gives you and your pretty boots the hairy eyeball. But he's all the way across the room, so you ignore him.

"Pass this to Cordelia," Xander says, handing you a piece of paper that has been mucho folded. His brown hair is flopping in more of a planned floppy way than its usual Xander-doesn't-care-about-his-hair floppy way.

"I might. If you tell me what it says," you say. His face goes a little pale, and a wave of alarm rushes through you. You were just kidding, but that face Xander's making? It is a face that tells you the note contains something mushy, something that no XY type would want to admit to writing, except to the XX he was writing it to. But Xander writing something like that to Cordelia? That is so wrong, so unthinkable, so . . . totally none of your business. You take pity. You lean across the aisle and whisper, "Cordy."

She doesn't turn her head. She keeps on chatting away with the assorted cheerleaders and rich girls who form the court of Queen Cordelia. "Cordy," you say again, but a loud *bwack* from the microphone on the stage drowns you out.

Principal Snyder gives the microphone a couple of taps that echo through the room and through your brain. Ouchies. Worst sound in the world. "Settle down people, settle down," Snyder yells into the mike even though it's on. It's far too early for such loudness.

Willow rushes in and grabs the seat next to you. "Unavoidable lateness. Bad faucet in the bathroom. Water. Pants. Did I miss anything?"

"Will, it's a school assembly. In the history of all school assemblies, was there ever anything that couldn't be missed?" Xander asks.

"We're only at 'settle down, settle down,'" you tell

her. "We haven't even gotten to the threats yet."

"Detention for anyone who does not settle down immediately," Principal Snyder threatens. The short little men. You've observed that they do love to threaten.

You hand Xander's note to Willow. "Will you pass this to her highness from Xander? I could not get her to acknowledge me."

"And you think I'll be able to?" Willow protests. But she stretches her hand across the aisle. "Um, Cordelia, from Xander." Cordelia gives a long trill of laughter with a flip of her long brown hair. The laugh–hair flip combo may or may not be related to Willow and/or the note.

Xander reaches across you and takes the note back. "Forget it. I just wanted to ask her about the assignment in history. I'll ask someone else."

You have a great internal lie detector. And, *boing!* It just went off.

"I'm very pleased to announce that we have a very special guest," Principal Snyder says.

Boing! Your lie detector just went off again. Principal Snyder is not at all pleased. He is another word that starts with p and ends with issed.

"The mayor has arranged for Ms. Victoria Belakane, founder of the Be the Ultimate You! program, to visit the school and help you students with your self-esteem issues," the principal continues.

"She came on the right day," Xander mutters, fingering the unaccepted note.

"If you ask me, getting rejected by Cordelia should build *up* your self-esteem," you tell him, while giving up a few claps for Ms. Whoever. Ms. Whoever, who has some very pointy-toed boots of her own. She looks like she's a gym bunny, except "bunny" sounds way too round and soft. This woman has the body fat of a greyhound.

"Hello, I'm Ms. Belakane, and I'm here to help each of you discover your strength," the woman says. Her big, dark Christina Ricci saucer eyes seem to be able to look everywhere at once. "Because when you find your strength, you find your self-esteem."

You don't need to hear this. Your self-esteem is just fine, thank you very much. Besides, you're tired from patrolling last night. One of the grave-poppers was especially feisty. And you had to get in some Angel time, of course. So sleep would be much better for you than psycho blah-blah.

"Buffy, do you think . . ." Willow lets her words trail off.

You open your eyes. "Do I think what?"

"Sometimes it seems like that guy, Oz, the one with the red hair and the Andersen's Pea Soup T-shirt . . . sometimes it seems like he kinda . . . looks at me. But I could be completely delusional. I mean, why would he look at me?"

Clearly, you need to give a mini self-esteem workshop of your own. "Because you're adorable. Look at you, with your shiny red hair and your kitten sweater. And because you're brilliant. And you're sweet. And"—

you glance over and Cordy and the Clones—"you're a total original."

"Eyes forward, mouths shut," Principal Snyder snaps as he passes you in his patrol of the auditorium.

You obey. You cannot afford detention. "For example, if you take the test and are ranked as a Smartie, the brain is your thing," Ms. Belakane is saying. "And how great is that!" She punches her fist in the air. Which is something no one over eight should ever attempt. Especially someone over eight wearing her hair in a bun. Even a bun that makes her look kinda schoolteacher dominatrix hot. *Wait*. Did you actually just think that? And then an even more disturbing thought occurs to you. "Um, there's a test involved?" you ask.

"Yeah, I heard we all have to take it at lunch," Xander answers. "It's to find out what qualities we can feel good about ourselves for having." He opens his brown eyes wide and gives you a big look-Ma-no-cavities smile. It's frightening.

"Tests plus Buffy never equals good feelings," you say. "Tests plus Buffy during Buffy's sacred lunchtime equals extreme crankiness."

"I might need another number-two pencil," Willow mutters. "I have three, but sometimes I sorta press down a little too hard when I'm filling in the bubbles and there is snappage."

Occasionally you still find it hard to believe that you have become actual friends with someone who enjoys number-two pencils and notebooks and those other studying accessories as much as you enjoy . . . actual accessories.

You return your gaze to Ms. Belakane, she of the sucking-the-joy-out-of-lunch. "I know your school has had more than its share of tragedy—murders, accidental deaths, suicides. And it is my privilege to bring my Be the Ultimate You! system to you, because I feel that you students need it more than anyone."

"Because we're such incredible losers," Xander says. "Thanks, lady."

"And I look forward to meeting each and every one of you to discuss the strengths I know you have within." Ms. Belakane does another fist pump. "Thank you!"

You glance at the clock. A miracle has occurred. You've been released a whole ten—count 'em, ten—minutes before the bell is supposed to go off. Principal Snyder is scurrying toward the mike. But it's too late. Everyone took that thank-you as a good-bye and is heading for the doors.

"I need to hit the library," you tell Willow and Xander. "I had one of my dreams last night. You know, the kind that come true."

"So you need Giles to put on his turban and interpret," Xander guesses.

"Yup. 'Cause this is a weird one," you say.

"I'll come with," Willow volunteers. "Maybe there will be research." Her green eyes visibly sparkle at the thought.

"Ooh, research. Last refuge of the terminally

unhip," Cordelia interrupts, pushing her way into your little convo-circle. "Count me out."

"No one ever counted you in," you tell her. "So, guys, are we library bound?"

"No," says Cordelia. Did she not hear you say she was uninvited? Why is she still here?

"I'm gonna, uh, do something else too," Xander says. Heroically, he manages to ask, "Unless, is the dream thing . . . does it require instantaneous action?"

"Not until I get the lowdown from Giles," you tell him. "Go do that other thing."

But he's already gone. And so is Cordelia. You and Willow watch their quickly retreating backs. You try not to think about Xander's note and what was in it.

"Library, remember?" Willow nudges you.

"Right. Library. Home of Watcher. Interpreter of Dreams." You lead the way to the library and right over to Giles, who's behind the checkout desk.

"I had one of the Dreams last night," you tell him. "Short version: Lucky from the Lucky Charms box was after me. Except he was about eight feet tall. And not a cartoon. And he never said anything was magically delicious. And he seemed to want to kill pretty much everyone, including me."

Giles does that thing where he frowns and blinks and acts like his English and your English are two different languages. "Lucky Charms?" he finally manages to say.

"Tasty cereal with toasted oats and colored marshmallows," Willow jumps in, playing interpreter. "Green clovers, pink hearts, blue moons . . . oh, and also, fortified with twelve vitamins and minerals."

Giles's frown gets frownier. "Forget the Lucky Charms," you tell him. "All you need to know is giant leprechaun. Much killing."

"Leprechauns don't in fact exist," Giles says. "But there is a demon that might look like a large one to the uninformed."

You try not to snort. Uninformed. Giles has never even heard of Lucky Charms. Who's the uninformiest?

"I believe that what you encountered in your dream was a Sleaninhnam demon," Giles explains. "They're very rare."

"As are leprechauns," you reply.

He blinks at you some more. "Yes. Well. Sleaninhnams are extremely dangerous, not to be taken lightly. I'll need to do some research on their weaknesses and fighting techniques."

"Oooh. With me!" Willow cries.

"Of course." Giles smiles at her. "I do know they are nasty creatures," he goes on. "They kill for sport, usually jumping rapidly back and forth between dimensions, which makes them tricky to fight."

"Fun," you say.

Giles ignores the sarcasm. "Meet me here at lunch," he says. "We'll need to do some agility training before you meet the Sleaninhnam—which will be soon, if your past dreams are any indicators."

"As long as I don't have to pronounce it to kill

it," you say. "But we'll have to train after school. Principal Snyder has scheduled an all-school love-in for lunch."

"I beg your—"

"We all have to take a test to help us with our self-esteem," Willow interrupts.

"Oh. Yes, right. I received a memo," Giles replies. "A test that encourages you teenagers to classify your-selves into narrowly defined roles. As if you don't do that to excess already. Cheerleader, brain, stoner, geek. Do I have it right?"

"Not bad for an old British guy," you tell him. The bell rings. "So, agility after school?"

"Hmm. Well. If you can't evade the test . . . Yes, but you'll have to be prompt; I need to leave at four." Giles takes off his glasses and polishes them, though as far as you could tell, they were spotless. "You see, Jenny Calendar and I—"

"You and Miss Calendar have a date?" you squeal, sounding perhaps a bit too much like the cheerleader you used to be.

"Not precisely. Coffee was mentioned."

"In-school coffee or out-of-school coffee?" Willow asks.

"We spoke of the shop around the corner," he admits, with a faint blush.

Outside coffee, plus evasiveness and blushing. You look at Willow, and together you say, "It's a date."

"Oh, very well." Giles replaces his glasses. "Buffy,

I don't like to encourage you to neglect school tasks, but perhaps you could find a way to . . ."

"Blow off the test that will teach me how to feel all warm and fuzzy when I think about myself?" you ask.

"Your self-esteem has always appeared to me to be quite adequate. And you have never faced a Sleaninhnam demon before. I don't want you patrolling unprepared," Giles answers. "Now run along or you'll both be late to class."

You and Willow run along. You meet back up by Willow's locker right before what would usually be lunch but what today will be a test or training. Which isn't really a tough decision. You don't want to go after that Sl— Sl— That big, red-haired, green-suited demoney thing without the training Giles thinks you need. And it's not just because the training doesn't involve annoying little bubbles and scratchy pencils. No, it's—

"Miss Summers. Miss Rosenberg." You know that voice. It's the voice of the head leprechaun himself, Principal Snyder. "I thought I would escort you ladies to the auditorium for the test," he says. "Miss Summers, I'm especially concerned with *your* self-esteem. I think that perhaps you've been feeling bad about yourself because of your tendencies toward delinquency."

"Nope," you assure him. "I'm very comfortable with my delinquency."

He's not amused. He's never amused. He just

crosses his arms and gives you the eye. You know what that expression means: It's either the test or detention. But Giles is waiting for you.

What should you do?

SLAYER CHOICE:
Do you decide to . . .

\ claim Willow's sick and say you have to take her home, so you can blow off the Ultimate You! personality test and train with Giles during lunch? *If yes, turn to page 12.*

\ blow off training and take the Ultimate You! personality test during lunch? The wrath of Snyder is more threatening than the wrath of Giles. *If yes, turn to page 66.*

"I really want to work on my low self-esteem. It's been keeping me up at night. Truly," you tell Principal Snyder. "But Willow is sick. And I have to take her home."

You look at Willow. She makes a halfway decent sick face. If she were wearing your boots, she'd be able to look in pain much more easily. But Willow is all about the sensible footwear.

"I suggest you take Miss Rosenberg to the nurse's office. That is what the nurse and her office are there for," Principal Snyder tells you, his eyes all narrowed.

"We were just there," you answer. He'll probably find out the truth eventually. But you'll deal with eventually . . . eventually. "It seems that Willow's sickness is the kind where she needs lots of sleep in her own bed. And she's kinda wobbly on her feet." You take Willow's arm. "The nurse didn't think it was safe for her to try to make it home on her own. And my self-esteem will severely plummet if I don't take her there."

"Because that would make her a bad friend," Willow adds helpfully.

Snyder stares at you. You stare right back. Always the best thing to do when you're lying. "Fine. Go," he finally says.

And you go. Straight to the library.

"Lying and sneaking accomplished," you tell Giles.

"I helped," Willow says proudly. "I'm a bad girl. Oh, yeah." She giggles, ruining any bad girl vibe she had goin'. Which, sorry, Will, wasn't much. Tip: When you have to say you're a bad girl, you probably aren't one.

"I've pulled out some likely texts where information on the Sleaninhnam may be found," Giles tells Willow. "It would be very helpful if you—"

Before the words are out of his mouth, Willow has her butt in a chair and her nose in one of the books. You and Giles head off to train.

The training room? Big mess. Piles of books. Rolled-up mats. Groups of chairs. There is hardly enough space to walk. "Giles, I'm not going to bother buying you nice things if this is the way you're going to treat them," you say, because that's what your mother always says when your bedroom is a mess.

"Because the Sleaninhnam will be appearing and disappearing into and out of dimensions, perhaps very rapidly, I want to concentrate on your footwork," Giles tells you. "So we'll do your usual fighting routine while moving through the obstacles."

"Okay, but you have to say nice things to me the whole time," you answer.

He raises his eyebrows.

"Because of all the self-esteem I'm missing out on," you explain as you do a perfect roundhouse kick over a pile of books.

SLAYER ACTION:
Turn to page 14.

"**T**he self-esteem lady has a problem. And it isn't self-esteem," Xander complains. "I'm guessing it's something that has to be treated by several sessions of electroshock therapy. The questions on that test could not have come from a healthy mind."

You check your watch. Xander has been ranting for eleven minutes, from the second he stepped foot in the library after school. And he hasn't even started to repeat himself. Impressive.

"'How many times do you chew your food?' And then the next question is some math problem that probably three people in school can figure out. And then that scratch-and-sniff section?" Xander shakes his head.

"'Scratch and sniff'?" Giles repeats. He sounds appalled.

"There was math?" Willow asks. She sounds jealous.

"And she stands up in front of everyone like everything she's saying and doing is perfectly normal," Xander rants on.

"You've just described half the teachers at this school," you tell him.

"No, she's worse. Because she claims to be all about caring, and helping, and wanting you to have a better life," Xander answers. "I don't like it."

"Caring. Helping. I don't like it either. Let's run her out of town," you say.

"And when do you find out what your classification is?" Giles asks.

"I have to meet with Ms. Bel-insane in fifteen minutes. One-on-one. If she's never seen again, you can't repeat any of this conversation to the police." Xander points at each of us in turn as he fails to look menacing.

"We should do something fun tonight to take away the badness," Willow suggests. "How about the Bronze?"

"Hmmm. Didn't I see a poster for Dingoes Ate My Baby that said they're playing at the Bronze tonight?" you ask. "And doesn't Oz play with the Dingoes?"

"There you go again." Giles throws up his hands.

"Didn't understand any of that, huh?" Xander asks him.

"Not a word." Giles disappears into his office.

Willow blushes. And when she blushes, with that pale skin, she really blushes. "Really? The Dingoes are playing?" She tries to sound innocent. "Who knew? What a coincidence. Does Oz play with them? Does my voice sound funny to you?"

"Yes." You wrap your arm around Willow's shoulder. "You and Xander should definitely go."

"I'm in," Xander says.

"But what about you, Buffy?" Willow asks.

"There's the green demon on the loose," you say. "He could show up at any time. I should probably patrol tonight."

"All night?" Willow sounds anxious. She could use some moral support at the Oz-fest, and Xander probably won't cut it, what with his being a guy and all.

But still, patrolling is your job. What to do?

SLAYER CHOICE:

Do you decide to . . .

❚ go patrolling? *If yes, turn to page 149.*

❚ go to the Bronze and hear the Dingoes? *If yes, turn to page 17.*

The Bronze is packed.

You make your way through the crowd and take a seat next to Willow and Xander. Cordelia is off slam dancing, with the emphasis on the slam. Although, slam dancing? So not the usual activity for perfect-hair Cordy, who throws a tizzy if she breaks a nail. So not the activity of anyone who has chosen to enter this decade with their dignity intact. Cordelia has obviously lost it.

Xander scoops up a handful of pretzels and shakes the empty bowl at a passing waitress. She grabs it on her way to the bar. Xander doesn't check out her butt in that I'm-not-checking-out-a-waitress's-butt-in-front-of-my-girl-type-friends way he usually does. But at least he's not checking out Cordelia's butt either. That note weirdness in the assembly this morning had you worried.

"Hey, kids!" Ms. Belakane sits down at your table like she's your bestest best friend. Excuse you. Why would any teacher type want to come to the Bronze? It's bizarre. "I ordered us some snacks," she says. "Have the Dingoes started to play yet? I want to show my support." Fist pump. Always with the fist pumps. Who told her that was okay?

Willow tells her they should be on in a few minutes. You couldn't have answered if you wanted to. Not that you wanted to. You're still trying to get over the fact that a near-teacher type is going all gal pal on you.

The waitress comes back with a bowl of pretzels and a plate of hamburgers and fries. Xander hoovers the pretzels before she has the chance to set them down on the table. Maybe he just wants his mouth full because he doesn't know what to say. You certainly don't. What topic is Ms. Belakane-appropriate?

"Uh, how did you come up with your self-esteem program?" you ask. Because you'd rather ask the questions than have her ask them. Who knows what she thinks is appropriate Bronze convo? Since she clearly has no appropriateness meter at all.

"I've always been interested in teenagers and the way they feel about themselves," Ms. Belakane says in her gravelly voice.

"So were you, like, low on the self-esteem when you were in high school?" Willow asks.

"I hardly remember high school," Ms. Belakane admits.

"Blocked it out, huh?" Xander asks through a bite of hamburger, if you can call half a burg a bite. Which you will. Just to be nice. Otherwise you'd have to call your friend Xander a big nasty hog-boy. A piece of bun falls out of his mouth and onto the floor. He reaches down and pops it back into his maw.

"Xander, the five-second rule is an at-home kind of rule. It's not really something that applies to public places with public shoes and other public nastiness," you tell him, even though it's too late because the piece of bun has already been swallowed.

"I think it's fine," Ms. Belakane murmurs, winking at Xander. She passes him some french fries. Then she gives a little squeal. There should be an age limit on squealing. And really, Ms. Belakane does not look like a squealer. She's too smooth and sleek and pulled together. You suspect the squealing is just her attempt to be down with today's teens.

"Oz, over here," Ms. Belakane calls. Inviting him to the table of you, Willow, and Xander. But she has to be forgiven in this case, because of Willow and the joy that is sure to follow an Oz appearance.

"Hey," Oz says. Oz is pretty much a one-word-response guy. But in his head, you suspect there are a lot more words going on. Which is good. Because Willow also has a lot of brain, with many words stored therein. But she's not using any of them right now. She's just kinda staring into space. Maybe it's her way of acting casual in front of the boy she likes.

Oz grabs a burger. He takes off the bun. Then he breaks off a piece of meat, reaches across the table—and feeds it to Ms. Belakane. And she lets him!

You have no words for the craziness. Cordelia, Xander, Oz . . . and this teacher lady. All crazy.

Did you enter the Bronze through the bizarro door?

SLAYER ACTION:
If you are at the Bronze to hang with Willow and Xander, turn to page 20.

If you are at the Bronze to see Giles and Ms. Belakane on a date, turn to page 213.

Oz feeds Ms. Belakane another bite of hamburger. It's rare, and a thin trail of blood drips down the pale skin of her chin. Oh, gross. There should be a better word. And there probably is. But you don't spend a lot of time thumbing through the dictionary because of the patrolling, and the staking, and the sending back to hell. Not that you'd probably do all that much thumbing, anyway.

You have the impulse to grab a napkin and wipe the blood away. But you're not going to become one of the servants to Ms. Belakane, even if the blood is yucking you out. You look over at Willow. She's staring at Oz like she's trying to decide if it's him or his evil twin. Then she picks up a french fry and holds it tentatively in Oz's direction. He doesn't notice. Which is good. Because the next move after mumbling "Hi, what's up?" probably shouldn't be feeding french fries. Or any other foodstuffs, for that matter. Willow eats the fry herself, her eyes all sad.

You kick Xander to try to get him to notice the sad eyes, but he doesn't even flinch. Or look in your direction. He's too busy scarfing down another burger. Cordelia better not have started him on the road to an eating disorder with her ignoring of his note or you'll have to . . . well, you'll have to sit her down and give her a good talking-to, that's what you're going to have to do.

A hand settles on your shoulder. You know that hand. You love that hand. You glance up, and Angel is standing there. All big and gorgeous and broody. And yours. You try to keep your smile mostly on the inside, because Willow and Xander don't have someone to smile at, not the kind of smile you smile at Angel.

"Well, how nice. Someone else to join our party," Ms. Belakane says. She licks the blood off her chin and reaches out her hand to Angel. Which means he has to take his hand off your shoulder so he can shake hers. Your skin feels lonely without his hand there.

"Sit down, please," Ms. Belakane cries. "We're all friends here."

No. You're not. But that would be rude to say, so you don't, you just think it. Angel sits down next to you. Which is also next to Ms. Belakane.

"Are you one of the teachers at Sunnydale High? I haven't met everyone yet," Ms. Self-Esteem asks.

Now Willow's sad eyes are sad for you. *Way to remind everyone that Angel's too old for me, lady,* you think. A couple of centuries too old for you. You try not to think about that, and you definitely try not to remind Angel of that. You glance at him, nervous. Did Ms. Belakane make him broodier?

Nope. He's smiling.

"No, I'm not a teacher. I'm—no, I'm not," Angel answers. And he keeps smiling at her. Angel smiles, like, once a week. And all those smiles should be at you. Not at a weird peppy grown-up lady inappropriately hanging with students. "And who are you?"

"I'm the creator of the Be the Ultimate You! program," Ms. Belakane says. "It's designed to help teenagers build their self-esteem."

"Right. Ms. Belakane's at our school to make sure everyone's feeling happy, happy, joy, joy all the time," you tell him. You let the snark creep into your voice. There's no reason to kiss up to Ms. Belakane, after all. As long as you're not being totally rude, it's all right to be sarcastic. Isn't it?

"That's sweet," Angel says. No snark. You don't think Angel has ever used the word "sweet." In all his two hundred and however many years. You stare at him. He looks normal. For a vampire with a soul.

"Thank you," Ms. Belakane purrs. "I do like to make everyone feel good."

Your mouth drops open. Did she really just say that? Wait, is she *flirting* with your boyfriend?

"A lot of kids have self-esteem issues," Angel says. "They're lucky to have someone like you to help them out."

Is *Angel* flirting with *her*? And did he just call you and your friends "kids"? You are not enjoying this new level of weirdness.

Xander flags down the waitress. "Can we get another round of everything, pretzels included?" he asks. "And maybe a couple chocolate milk shakes." He glances around the table. "Anyone else need anything to drink?"

The waitress raises her eyebrows but doesn't comment, just jots down Xander's order and a couple more sodas for the rest of you. Then she grabs the empty plates and hurries away.

"Um, Oz," Willow says. He doesn't seem to hear

her. He's too busy rolling the salt and pepper shakers over and over on their sides while he stares at Ms. Belakane. "Oz," Willow tries again.

"Huh?" he asks without taking his eyes from Ms. Belakane.

"Your band, they seem to be wanting you up onstage," Willow tells him, gesturing up at the Dingoes.

"Oh." Oz gets up and ambles away without a good-bye.

"He's apparently not so much with the silly chitchat," you say, to make Willow feel better. She smiles at you, but it's one of those smiles that isn't really a smile. You can tell she's freaked by the Ms. Belakanity of the evening too. Does Oz have a crush on this teacher lady?

Does Angel?

"I'm going to go to the little girls' room. I want to make sure I'm back before they start to play," Ms. Belakane says.

Little girls' room. Please. You're surprised she didn't use the word "tinkle."

"She's really sweet," Angel says, his eyes on Ms. Belakane as she walks away.

Twice with the "sweet" in one day? What kind of insane mojo does Ms. Belakane have to make everyone act so weird around her?

You think about following her just to see what she does. And maybe even to have a little chat with her about how flirting with a girl's boyfriend or crush isn't so great for the self-esteem of said girl.

But on the other hand, Angel is here. And he's beautiful. And you love him. And Ms. Belakane is gone. What better opportunity are you going to have to steal him away for some quality alone time?

SLAYER CHOICE:

Do you decide to . . .

\ follow Ms. Belakane to the ladies' room to see what her deal is? *If yes, turn to page 121.*

\ take Angel somewhere private to make out with him? *If yes, turn to page 25.*

Y ou slide up close to Angel. "I think I saw a big, bad vamp out in the alley. Want to help me check it out?" you whisper in his ear.

Angel manages to pull his eyes away from the sweet, sweet Ms. Belakane as she heads for the bathroom. You take his hand and lead him across the dance floor and out the side door. His eyes flick back and forth and his muscles tense as he readies himself for a fight. "I don't see anything," he says.

You step right in front of him and stare into his face. "I do," you say. "I see my boyfriend. And I see that my boyfriend is now alone with me."

Angel doesn't smile. But he's never much with the put-on-a-happy-face, so that's not unusual. What *is* unusual is that he doesn't move the one inch that separates the two of you and put his arms around you and make you feel all squishy inside. Didn't he hear you making a point of the two of you being in the aloneness together?

He heads back toward the door. "Wait!" you cry.

He turns around. "There's nothing out here," he tells you.

"Fighting the baddies isn't the only use of a dark and somewhat smelly alley," you reply. Angel seems to be made up of big chunks of denseness today. "We can also use it to do something with lips. Two pairs of them."

He stares at you blankly.

You consider grabbing him and kissing him. But that seems too pathetic. You try something else. "Do you like my boots?" Your piggies squeal in protest as you wiggle your toes at him. And you realize that talking about the boots might be equally pathetic.

Without a word, Angel walks back into the Bronze.

You decide not to follow him. Because that would be even more pathetic.

Your boyfriend just flirted—kinda—with Ms. Belakane, and then didn't want to make out with you.

There's only one thing left to do.

Go home and hide in bed.

SLAYER ACTION:
Turn to page 27.

"**O**h, Buffy, you're home," your mom calls as you come through the door. "You've got to see this." You drag yourself into the living room and sit on the edge of the sofa. Your mother is watching Letterman. Letterman is watching a pug dog. "Lieeee uuuuh ooooh," the dog cries.

This day has been too strange. You don't want to see dogs singing.

"Doesn't it sound exactly like it's saying 'I love you'?" your mom asks. "I was flipping toward the Discovery Channel and I had to stop."

"Liieee uuuuh ooooh," the dog cries again.

It does sound freakishly like it's saying "I love you." But you've had enough of the freakish for one day. And the forecast for tomorrow is many more inches of freakishness. "I going to go to night-night." You kiss the top of your mother's head. You manage to make it up the stairs and into your pajamas.

"No dreams," you order yourself as you climb under the covers. You want eight hours of nice and normal before the lunacy starts again.

SLAYER ACTION:
Turn to page 28.

Your weather forecast was wrong. You didn't get inches of freak today. You got a freak storm, with possibly a tidal wave of the freaky on the way. You survey the scene around the lovely green lawn outside Sunnydale High.

Xander is having a picnic. A picnic without a blanket, or a basket, or paper plates, or plastic silverware . . . or other people. His picnic consists of paper bags full of food. And him. And his two hands.

The school's most notable burnout and this girl who you're pretty sure is the head of the Junior Achievers Club—there was an awards assembly that you think was for her and some sort of record she broke, but you were really sleepy that day, so maybe it was someone else—are sitting close together on a nearby bench.

Harmony is doing gymnastics on the grass. You notice she has a black eye, which she hasn't even attempted to cover up with concealer—a sign of the apocalypse if ever you saw one, and you've seen many.

Dave Ryder, who only shows up in your history class a couple of times a week, sits in front of the vending machine near the cafeteria door. As far as you can tell, he thinks it's a slot machine. He's just camped out there, pumping in quarters, one after the other. And eating the candy as fast as it comes out.

Brian Williams, in his beloved DEBATERS DO IT FASTER T-shirt, heads over to the machine. He peers through the glass, then a flush creeps up his neck and onto his face. "You ate the last Mars bar?" he yells. Dave doesn't even look up from playing the candy slots. He just keeps feeding his machine the quarters, like any minute it's going to spew all the candy it has left.

"Dave, I asked you if you ate the last Mars bar." Brian grabs candy lover Dave by the hair and smashes his head into the machine. The glass cracks, and blood drips down Dave's head. He seems to notice Brian for the first time.

"Do you want a Mars bar?"

"Yes!" Brian cries.

Dave starts making retching noises as if he's going to yuke. You can't believe him. He's making jokes when Brian just shoved his head through a glass plate? You run across the grass to them. You jerk Dave out of the way and shove Brian against the candy machine. "We do not bash people's heads in because they have eaten a candy bar we want," you explain to him. "Now are you going to go away, or am I going to have to put you inside the candy machine for a time-out?"

Brian glares at you. Then he turns and walks away.

"He just wanted a Mars bar," Dave says mildly. He slides up in front of the machine again. "It's broken," you tell him. He sticks in more quarters anyway. No candy falls into the tray. Dave stares at the empty tray for a moment. Then he presses his hand against the cracked glass until it breaks. He pulls a candy bar free and eats it with his bleeding fingers.

"You want some candy?" he asks.

"Uh, no thanks," you say, retreating. Dave has turned out to be more of a chocoholic than you expected. You wonder where Willow is. You really need to see Willow right now. You could use an assist. If Willow is still Willowish. Because nobody else is acting like themselves today.

Cordelia walks by with Emily Eiselin from the Young Businesswomen Club. They're talking about kickboxing. But how do they even know each other?

You hear someone crying behind you. You turn around. It's Oz. "What's wrong?" you exclaim. He holds out his hand, and you see a baby bird. Very baby. It looks almost embryonic. All thin skin and veins. Gently, you touch its head. "I don't know if there's anything we can do for it, Oz. It's just too young."

Oz gives a choked sob. "But I'm a Mommie. It's my job. I can't let it die. It's my job to keep it safe and warm until it can take care of itself. I'm a Mommie."

There is no proper response to a wild-haired musician telling you he's a bad mother, you find.

A shriek comes from across the lawn. Harmony, Cordy, and Emily are raising Amy Madison up the flagpole. "I, uh—" You look at Oz's devastated face. Then you catch sight of Xander. He's choking on what looks like half a bag of marshmallows that he's crammed into his mouth all at once. "Oz, I'll be back as soon as I can."

You dash toward Xander, trying to remember the Heimlich maneuver. "Hang on, Amy!" you shout over your shoulder. "You're next!"

SLAYER ACTION:

If Angel was acting weird yesterday,
turn to page 32.

If Giles was acting weird yesterday,
turn to page 232.

"**W**eird weirdness, huh?" you ask Willow. She showed up in time to give Xander the Heimlich and assist Oz with the baby bird while you dealt with the other assorted madness, which required a hair-pulling fight with Cordelia. But your shift in the Sunnydale looney bin seems to be over—for now. So you head to your lockers.

"Yeah. And you know what was also weird?" Willow says. "I kinda liked it when Oz called himself a Mommie. Does that mean . . . ? What does that mean?"

"I think it just means you really like him," you answer. "At least Xander didn't do too much damage to himself with his little one-man smorgasbord."

"It's good he chose marshmallows instead of crackers. 'Cause I heard that with soda crackers, if you put enough in at once, they form this kind of mortar in your mouth and throat and it won't come back up no matter what you do," Willow says.

"So Xander would've been a mortarmouth?" you quip.

"Better than a mallowmouth." Willow opens her locker and loads up on the books. "Huh. I guess that's not really a pun."

"Do you think maybe the 'mallows were a cry for help?" you ask as you continue on to your locker. "He was eating well beyond the Xander daily requirements. Stress fueling?"

Willow puts her serious face on. "If I were Xander, I don't know if I'd be all that happy getting classified as a Teddie."

You frown. "You think this is all about that stupid Ultimate You! test? Would Xander really care that much about some dumb label?"

Willow shrugs. "Everyone else seems to be all label-obsessed today. I saw Harmony hanging out with Brian Williams. They're both Peppies."

"See, now with the way Harmony has been acting, I'd call her more Crazie than Peppie," you say.

"Yeah, but at least there're a lot of Peppies. Tons of people are aggressive. But Xander's a Teddie, which just means he's agreeable," Willow says. "Agreeable is . . . nice. Agreeable is good. But does anyone want to be told that agreeableness is their strongest quality? It's kinda . . . not much."

"And being labeled aggressive is?" you ask.

"If you're a cheerleader, getting classed as a Peppie is probably okay," Willow answers.

"True. They live to pep." You shake your head. "Wouldn't Xander tell us if he was an unhappy Teddie? That's the stuff he tells us. That's our role. He shouldn't be OD'ing on marshmallows. He should be reaching out for the support of non-Teddie, non-Peppie, non-Mommie friends like ourselves." You get to your locker and unload the books.

"Maybe he just had the hungries," Willow suggests.

The image of Dave eating candy with his bloody fingers flashes into your mind. "Well, we'll keep an eye on our Mr. Harris," you say. "I'm going to go patrol."

"Oh! Library!" Willow cries. "I want to go over my Sleaninhnam research with you. There's some need-to-know stuff."

"Later, okay?" you ask. "I think the weird weirdness might turn into bad badness. I need to see what I can find out." Plus, Angel is going to be waiting for you. You have a standing patrol date.

"It will just take a minute," Willow presses. "He's a pretty scary demon."

You think about it. Giles did say the Sleaninhnam was a nasty one. But you've taken on many a nasty before with no problem. And you really don't want to skip the chance to see Angel. You need to find out what was up with the flirting and the leaving at the Bronze last night. It's all you could think about today—well, whenever you weren't dealing with the pervasive insanity at school.

Is everything okay with you and Angel? You have to find out.

But is it worth skipping a demon-strategy session to get to Angel five minutes sooner?

SLAYER CHOICE:

Do you decide to . . .

❧ go with Willow to the library? *If yes, turn to page 35.*

❧ go straight out to patrol—and meet Angel? *If yes, turn to page 141.*

It's very hard to resist Willow when she's in plead mode. And even though the weird weirdness could turn into bad badness, you might just run into that Sl—Sl—that big ol' leprechaun. You should be responsible. You should be prepared. Wait. The voice in your head just started to sound like Giles. You concentrate hard on Willow's cute hairband in order to banish the Giles from your mind. It works.

"To the library," you tell Willow. She gives a happy bounce. Which is nice to see. Maybe helping Oz with his baby bird cheered her up.

"I wonder how Giles's date went yesterday," you say as the two of you head to the library. "He couldn't even say the word 'date,' so I don't know how he could actually have one."

"I think he and Ms. Calendar make a cute couple," Willow answers. "They have all the magick knowledge in common." She frowns. "But in order to get with Ms. Calendar, he's going to have to accept the fact that civilized human beings do actually use computers."

Willow opens the library doors, taking a deep breath of the musty smell of all those pages of old paper. She complains of Giles's computerphobia and she's as whiz-bangey on the keyboard as Ms. Calendar. But she grooves on the ancient paper smell as much as he does. The love of old books, you'll never understand it. But Willow would wear it as a perfume. If they made Eau de Old Book, that is, which you're hoping they don't.

You like new smell. New car. New shoes. New anything.

Except for Angel. He's old, and you like him just fine.

You push open the library doors and look around. It's deserted. "Giles?" you yell.

No answer. No Giles. That never happens.

You raise your eyebrows at Willow.

"You don't think they're having coffee *again*, do you?" she asks in a hushed tone.

"I dunno. That would be moving pretty fast for Giles," you say.

"Well, I can tell you everything we found out about the Sleaninhnam demon," Willow says. "We don't need Giles." She starts toward a pile of dusty leather books. "Wait. Don't tell him I said that," she adds.

You nod.

"Okay," Willow starts, "like Giles said, the Sleaninhnam demon opens portals and jumps from dimension to dimension fighting with people. And demons. And whatever else is in other dimensions. What's in other dimensions?"

You shrug. All you know about other dimensions is that they send bad things here way too often. So they must be bad. You've heard Giles use the words "hell dimension," which also sounds bad.

"So he's a jumpy interdimensional killing machine," you sum up.

"Yeah. But he doesn't just kill for fun. Although he might enjoy it. This book"—she pulls a leather-bound one with gold lettering out from the pile she'd been

working on earlier—"explains that the Sleaninhnam
gets the power he uses to dimension-jump through
killing."

"So no killing, no jumping," you say.

"Right." Willow sets the book aside. "I found out
some cool stuff about his home world, but nothing
vital. You want to hear?"

"Angel is meeting me at the cemetery—," you
begin.

"You don't want to hear," Willow interrupts.
"But there's one more thing. I found an old Latin
Sleaninhnam reference that has some fighting tips for
you, but I didn't finish translating the whole thing. Let
me read it really fast."

She picks a skinny yellow book off the top of the
pile and turns to a page she has marked.

"Hey, does the leprechaun—," you start.

"It's a Sleaninhnam demon."

"Yeah. Does he speak with an accent?" you ask.
"Like . . . 'top o' the mornin' to ya'?"

Willow looks up from the page she's trying to
read. "Um, Buff, he comes from another dimension,
not Ireland."

"So that would be no?" you ask.

Willow nods. "Why?"

You shrug. "I just like those accents."

Willow reads. You try to imagine Angel with one
of those accents. He comes from Ireland. You wonder
if he would do one for you. Doubtful.

You wonder if he would do one for Ms. Belakane.

You really need to get out there and find your boyfriend. You have to make sure everything's okay. You have to make sure he still loves you. "Will, is this gonna take long?" you ask.

"Ah. I knew there was going to be something good in this part!" Willow says, ignoring you. "You are going to be so glad you came."

"He *does* have an accent?"

Willow ignores you. "Listen to this. It isn't accurate that the Sleaninhnam gets power from killing. He gets power from *fighting*. He kills because, when beings know they are going to die, that's when they fight the hardest."

"So that's when the thing in green gets the most juice," you say.

"And not just power to dimension-jump, at least according to this book. He gets strength in general," Willow explains.

"Which means that to fight him, I can't fight him," you say. "Because if I fight him, he'll get stronger and stronger."

"Hold on, hold on," Willow mutters. "Compliments!"

You don't think you've ever heard Willow ask for a compliment before. But hey, she deserves them. "That headband looks really good with your hair," you tell her. "It makes the color—"

"Not me. The Sleaninhnam demon. That's how you kill him. Don't fight him. Compliment him," Willow explains.

You stare at her for a few seconds. "Are you sure you translated that right?" you ask.

"Yes." She sounds offended.

"So I say 'My, what a big mallet you have' and the demon dies?" you ask. This does not sound like a good plan.

"Well, you might have to compliment him more than once," Willow tells you.

"And he dies?"

"Eventually. It's like the reverse of fighting him. You fight him, he gets stronger. You compliment him, he gets weaker."

"Wow. I've heard of not being able to take a compliment . . . ," you joke. Then you smile at Willow. "Thanks for doing the book work. I'm going to go—"

"Have smoochies with Angel," Willow says.

"And patrol," you agree. But you're hoping for smoochies. You're hoping last night at the Bronze was all some bad—and strange—dream.

You wave good-bye to Willow and rush over to the cemetery as fast as you can. Angel usually meets you by the angel statue in the little courtyard. You expect him to be there already, since you're late because of Willow's Sleaninhnam tutorial. You jog into the courtyard, excited to see him.

He's not there.

You stop, your heart sinking. Is he just late? You wait around for a few minutes. But still no Angel.

Something came up, you tell yourself. He's late. He'll be here.

But you can't wait around all night. You're here to patrol. Sunnydale is a bastion of weirdness right now, and the big green demon is out there somewhere. Angel will just have to come find you.

You check to make sure you have a stake in the inside pocket of your leather coat. Not for Angel. For the vamps who aren't your b-friend. You start walking through the tombstones, looking for fresh graves.

Your Slayer sense prickles. You have the feeling someone is watching you. Angel? You turn. No Angel. No one at all.

You continue through the cemetery, walking under a cluster of elm trees. And you get that eyes-on-your-back feeling again. This time you spin around and drop into a fighting stance. There's a faint glow of yellow light. But no one's there.

You turn back around—and hello! An eight-foot-tall leprechaun is standing in front of you. He looks like the Incredible Hulk. Well, except his skin isn't green. Just his velvet suit and his top hat. He holds a humongous wooden mallet. A mallet that is whizzing down toward your head.

You drop. You roll. Usually next you would leap to your feet and kick. Or punch. Or stake. But you can't fight. Not this time. "What a beautiful mallet!" you yell up at the Sleaninhnam demon. Because who else could it be?

"No, it isn't. It's old. It's falling apart!" the demon bellows. *Bam!* The mallet hits the ground next to your head. You spring up. A hole of light opens up, and the

Sleaninhnam slides down it on a golden beam.

You hear a whooshing sound behind you. You jump up, grab a branch of an elm, and swing your legs up and out to the side. The Sleaninhnam appears again, hefting the mallet above his head to hit you up in the tree.

You swing yourself over the branch, narrowly avoiding the mallet. You really want to fight this guy. He gives leprechauns a bad name, even if he isn't one. *Fighting makes him stronger,* you tell yourself. You repeat it over and over in your mind like a mantra as you scramble higher into the tree.

The last thing you want to do is make nice with His Greenness. But it's the only way to kill him. "I love your hair color," you call down from your perch. "It's so rich. I'm thinking of going red myself. Do you think I could have a picture to show my stylist?"

The Sleaninhnam's huge face is only a few feet below yours. You climb up another branch. You can compliment him from up here. The tree won't support his unjolly green giant self.

"You have a sassy mouth on you," the Sleaninhnam growls. He swings his mallet like an ax, pounding at the tree trunk. The whole tree shakes.

"And you have the most beautiful green eyes," you answer. "Plus, your cheeks are so rosy. I could just eat you up!"

The demon pulls back his mallet for another swing—and it falls out of his grip. He's obviously getting weaker. You try to think of something else you can say. "Love the suit. Love the hat. Love the gold buckles on the shoes. Love the whole ensemble," you shout.

Thud. The Sleaninhnam falls to the ground next to his mallet. You climb down a few branches. "You have eyelashes most girls would kill for." There's no reaction. Is that it? Is that all it took to kill the thing? You scramble down to the lowest branch and stare at the big green buttons on the demon's jacket.

You leap to the ground. "You make a beautiful corpse," you say.

Nothing. He doesn't even bother to say thank you.

You leave him there and go straight for the cemetery exit. An entire demon attack and your so-called boyfriend hasn't even shown up to help. That's not right. And you intend to do something about it. You head over to Angel's. He owes you a big-time explanation for why he was a no-show tonight. Not to mention why he blew you off at the Bronze last night. And *really* not to mention why he was so friendly with Ms. Belakane.

You knock on Angel's door. He opens it.

And he doesn't immediately start apologizing. You adjust your expression to make it absolutely clear that you are hurt. He still doesn't apologize. You remember that even though he is a vampire with heightened senses, he is still a guy. You probably need to use words. "Me. Cemetery. You. Where?"

"Oh. I forgot I was supposed to meet you," he says. And he doesn't move his big stupid self out of the doorway so you can get in. Also, he doesn't apologize.

"I had to fight a Sleaninhnam demon. By myself," you tell him.

He just looks at you. Unimpressed. Unapologetic. Like he has no idea what you're doing there or what you want from him.

"Do you have anything to say to me?" you ask. *Like, "I'm sorry" or "I love you,"* you add silently.

"Not really," Angel replies.

You open your mouth. Then close it again. What are you supposed to say to this cold, unfeeling person who's replaced your boyfriend?

"Okay, well, bye," Angel says. He shuts the door on you.

You stand there, staring at the wooden door two inches in front of your face. This has gone beyond Angel acting a little off. The guy you know and love would never close a door on you. Something's wrong. And when something's wrong, it usually means a supernatural something.

You have to find out what's really happening with Angel. But how?

SLAYER CHOICE:

Do you decide to . . .

❚ stake out Angel and see where he goes? *If yes, turn to page 156.*

❚ go find Willow and get her help figuring out Angel's behavior? *If yes, turn to page 44.*

All you can think about is getting to your best friend. Your world has just been flipped upside down. You wouldn't be surprised if chocolate now tasted like dirt. Willow is the only one who can help you make sense of things.

You run to her house and directly to the glass doors that lead to her bedroom. There's no way you want to deal with anything parental right now. You knock with both hands.

A second later, Willow is there, opening the doors and pulling you inside. "Buffy, what happened? Are you hurt?"

"Yes," you say as you flop down on her bed. You feel tears fill your eyes and you blink them away. "I don't know . . . I don't understand. . . ."

"What? Tell me."

At least Willow is the same. She let you in. She's saying all the right Willow things. "Angel . . . he . . ." You find it hard to find the right words. "He didn't meet me to patrol. So I went over there. And he didn't apologize or anything." You frown. That's still not it. "He didn't care. At all. That I had to fight the demon myself, or—"

"You fought the Sleaninhnam?" Willow interrupts.

"Yeah. And it was fine. The compliment thing completely worked," you say. "But Angel didn't ask anything about it. He was sending out these massive Buffy-leave vibrations, and I don't know why." You wait for Willow to say something, to come up with some great logical reason for Angel to act the way he did.

But Willow doesn't say anything for a long time. And all she comes up with then is, "Oh, Buffy."

"I know," you say. "It's like some light switch went off in him. Is he bored with me now? Is that it? He's known so many women, and I'm just this high school girl—"

"You are not just this high school girl," Willow interrupts. "You're the Slayer. And you're . . . *you*. He can't be bored of you. It's impossible."

Someone knocks on Willow's door. Through the curtains you see a large silhouette.

Willow catches her breath. "You did say you killed the Sleaninhnam, right?"

"Yeah." Still, Willow obviously wasn't expecting any large . . . someones . . . at her door. "Let me get it," you whisper. You creep over and whip the closest half of the door open. And you stand there, rooted to the ground in shock.

"Xander?" you croak.

"Xander?" Willow repeats. She sounds as freaked as you feel.

"Yeah, it's Xander," he says. He shoots you and Willow a who-did-you-think-it-was look. "Can I come in?"

"Sure." You back away from him, your eyes locked on his belly. His Santa Claus bowl full of jelly belly. Make that barrel full of jelly. Make that barrel full of some murky amber-colored gunk. The rolls of fat you can see coming out of the bottom of his sweatshirt don't exactly look like they are made of flesh.

"Doughnuts, anybody?" Xander pulls a box out of his backpack. Then another. And one more.

"No!" you almost shout.

"No!" Willow says at the same time.

"Goody. More for me." Xander sits down on the floor and starts to eat. One doughnut after the other, without taking even a second in between. After the third one, you can't take it. You sit down next to him and grab his wrist.

"You practicing for the county fair?" you ask gently.

"Huh?" Xander reaches with his free hand for a blue doughnut with red sprinkles. You kick the open box of doughnuts under the bed. Willow confiscates the two other boxes.

"Xander, uh, you've put on some weight in the last few . . . hours," Willow tells him. She gets up and opens her closet. There's a full-length mirror attached to the inside of the door.

You stand up and grab Xander by the hand. It takes a hard tug to get him to his feet now that he's gotten so heavy. You lead him over to the mirror and point him toward his own oh-so-strange image. You're expecting a cry of disgust. But Xander just pulls up his shirt, stares at his massive stomach, and goes, "Huh."

"I think you must have gained a hundred pounds in the last two days," you say.

"Yeah, and ninety of it was just since the end of school today," Willow adds.

Xander gives his translucent amber belly a tap. It

ripples. You wince. Willow backs away a step. Xander goes, "Huh." He still doesn't sound too worried. You hesitate. You don't want to freak him out. But with a stomach that size—and that color—he really *should* be freaking out.

"Maybe we should all go see Giles," Willow suggests.

"Good idea," you say. "Xander?"

"Okay," Xander agrees.

You make your way to Giles's apartment as quickly as possible, which isn't all that quickly. Partly because you're afraid that walking too fast might damage Xander somehow. And partly because Xander insists on a pit stop for snacks.

When Giles opens the door, you wonder for one horrifying second if Jenny Calendar might be there. But then you decide Giles couldn't be such a player that he could go from coffee to inviting a woman to his place in only two days.

"What seems to be the—" Giles's eyes land on Xander's stomach. "Ah. Come in." He ushers all of you into his living room. "Would you like anything to—perhaps that wouldn't be the best idea. Who would like to bring me up to the moment here?" He looks at Willow.

"We don't really know anything," she explains. "Xander just came by, to hang out, looking like that. He doesn't seem to be bothered by it."

You, Willow, and Giles look at Xander. He's eating Cheez Doodles and he gives you a bright orange smile. "Want some?" he asks, shaking the bag.

"No!" you all answer at once.

"Okay," Xander says, and keeps on munchin'.

"There have been other weirdnesses at school," you tell Giles. "Cordelia and the cheerleaders have become . . ." You look to Willow for help.

"Mean, nasty ho's," she suggests.

"No, something new. More aggressive. This girl came to school today wearing the same sweater as Cordy, and Cordy almost gouged her eyes out. I had to separate them," you tell Giles.

"Yeah, Cordelia and Harmony are picking fights all over the place," Willow adds. "But they don't even act like it's weird. They're all violent and peppy at the same time."

"Peppy. A Peppie. That's one of Ms. Belakane's Ultimate You! classifications, isn't it?" Giles asks.

"Yeah," you say. "In fact, I think Cordelia is a Peppie."

"So is Harmony," Willow says. "And Oz is a Mommie." Her eyes are wide with the realization. "Oh, my god—*that's* why he was so upset about the baby bird!"

You nod. It's all starting to make sense. Well, except for Angel's weird behavior. You try to shove that thought out of your mind. There are more important things to think about now—like Xander's disgusting stomach.

"A lot of people have been getting caught up in their Ultimate You! categories," you tell Giles. "Everyone's asking if you're a Smartie or a Peppie or a Mommie."

"You haven't seen any other physical changes, such as . . ." Giles nods at Xander.

"No," Willow says. "But Xander wasn't like this when we saw him in school today."

You feel a *click* in your head. "Do you think other people have changed too? Like maybe Cordelia has horns now or something?"

Willow shrugs.

"What was Xander's classification?" Giles asks.

"He's a Teddie," Willow says. "It means he's agreeable."

"Yup," says Xander.

Giles thinks for a moment. "It seems to me that we begin with researching demons who bring about these sorts of changes in their prey," he says.

But you have a better idea—one that will let you get to the bottom of Angel's strange behavior too. You hope. "I say we go after Ms. Belakane directly," you say. "This all started with her tests, right?"

"It seems that way," Giles admits.

"That's why nothing has happened to me and Buffy," Willow jumps in. "We didn't take the test. So, you know, no fatness or overpeppiness."

Or girlfriend-ignoriness, you add silently. You know Angel didn't take the Ultimate You! test. He's not a Peppie, or a Mommie, or a Smartie, or even a Teddie. But he's different. And it started when he met Ms. Belakane at the Bronze.

"Well," Giles says. "How do you want to handle this? I still feel that some research is in order. After all, even if we are to assume Ms. Belakane is behind the . . . behind Xander's . . . well, even if we assume that, we still don't know how it was accomplished."

"Or why." Willow wrinkles her nose a tiny bit as she looks at Xander.

"I'd rather just go after Ms. Belakane and see what she does," you say. "Research takes too long." *And I want my boyfriend back,* you think.

"But research showed you how to kill the Slean-inhnam demon," Willow points out. "So, see, research is your friend."

She's right. You know she's right. But you still want to go after Ms. Belakane immediately. What do you do?

SLAYER CHOICE:

Do you decide to . . .

❚ go find Ms. Belakane? *If yes, turn to page 159.*

❚ listen to Giles and Willow and research Ms. Belakane first? *If yes, turn to page 51.*

You think of the Sleaninhnam demon. If you'd skipped off to battle Mr. Not-So-Magically Delicious without doing research—okay, having Willow do research—you'd probably be one very dead Buffy right now. "Maybe doing research would be good," you say.

Giles looks pleased. Willow looks happy. Xander keeps eating.

"I could make tea," you suggest. Because research and you, not such great friends.

"That would be very useful, Buffy," Giles lies. "Thank you." He and Willow head over to the row of bookshelves. Xander follows you into the kitchen, shaking Doodle crumbs from the almost empty bag into his mouth.

You pour water into kettle, turn kettle on, put kettle on stove. You can cook! Xander pulls a box of cookies out of one of the cupboards. It says BISCUITS on the front, because Giles, always with the British. But you know they're really cookies.

"Xander, those might be for some special—"

Xander has already scarfed seven of them, so you don't bother to finish the sentence. You try something else. "Xan, what happened during your meeting with Ms. Belakane?"

"She told me I was a Teddie, and that Teddies are special because Teddies are agreeable and everyone likes Teddies, and that I should feel good about being a Teddie," Xander answers, with way too much chewage and way too little mouth closage. "And I do. I like being liked."

"But what about the part where the test was stupid, and Ms. Belakane should get electroshock therapy?" you ask.

Xander shrugs. "I dunno. I guess when Ms. Belakane explained it to me, it made more sense." He makes a cookie sandwich with one cookie in the middle of two others. He pops it in his mouth.

"Did you eat anything in her office?" you ask. "Or drink?"

"No. Does she have something good in there?" Xander makes a double-decker cookie sandwich—five cookies. You can't watch as he chokes it down. But you can hear his skin stretching, a sound like a finger running across a balloon as his stomach expands.

The teakettle lets out a piercing whistle, drowning out the sound. You almost don't want to take it off the stove. The sound is better than that stomach-stretching one. But you grab a potholder and pull it off the burner. Turn off the stove. Gather cups, tea bags, honey—

Which you have to take away from Xander, who has been pouring it straight down his gullet. He gives it up without protest and grabs a stick of butter from the fridge. Licking it like an ice-cream cone, he follows you to Giles's living room.

"We've begun to research demons that exercise mind control over their victims," Giles tells you. His eyes flick to Xander, then away. "There are several who use various sorts of mental coercion to form armies that they will use to bring about the apocalypse, that sort of thing. I can't see how our friend"—his eyes go to Xander again—"would be useful in that way."

"The cheerleaders are behaving somewhat army-esque. . . ."

"I found this one demon who used mind mumbo-jumbo to get him the largest harem in his dimension," Willow jumps in. "But also, so not Xander. Because he's a boy. And because of the jiggly belly. Unless, maybe the demon liked the bigness. It didn't say."

Xander takes a long, slurpy lick of his butter stick. His stomach gurgles, and a new bulge appears between the top of his sweatpants and the top of his sweatshirt.

"I can't . . . when I look . . ." Willow stops, then tries again. "When Xander and I were in the third grade we had to do a report on ants. Well, you could pick the insect, and we chose ants. And on the cover, we made an ant out of felt, with pipe-cleaner antennae and those plastic eyes that have little black pieces of plastic inside the clear plastic, so that the eyes can shake up and down, and—"

"Will," you say.

"Right, shaky eyes, not the point. But in the report? There was this part about honeypot ants. They are these ants that let other ants feed from their bodies. They gave me nightmares."

"Will," you say again.

"Right. It's just . . . Xander's tummy. It looks like those ants. It gives me the creepy crawlies." She turns to Xander, keeping her gaze on his face. "Not you. Just your . . . you know."

"Want some cookies?" Xander replies.

"No, thanks," she says.

"You may be on to something there," Giles tells Willow. "In ant communities there are also fighters who guard the colony and the queen, and nurturers who care for the eggs until they mature. That goes along with two of Ms. Belakane's categories, does it not?"

"The Peppies might as well be called the Warriors," you agree.

"And the Mommies are all about the nurturing," Willow adds.

Giles pulls a new group of books off his shelves. "Instead of demons with mind control, let's search for demons with antlike characteristics."

"Good plan." Willow grabs a new book and gets with the reading. Giles hands you a book too, although yours is much smaller than his or Willow's. Nobody bothers giving Xander a book.

And then with the quiet, and the book smell. Mixed with the butter smell. And the licking. You try to read. You do. But the studying and the researching, it makes you want to punch and kick.

Or else it makes you think about Angel. In the quiet, you can hear yourself telling him that you fought the demon alone. And you can hear him not caring. And it's so not about the demon. You've fought demons alone before. You're the Slayer. But Angel's your boyfriend. Isn't he? It's not like you've ever introduced him to anyone that way. And he certainly doesn't call himself that. But he treats you like he's your boyfriend.

Until tonight. When he treated you like you were the Avon lady.

You read a few more sentences. But they have nothing to do with ants or eating or crazy cheerleaders. Can't Willow and Giles just tell you what to go kill already? You want to hurt whatever did this to Xander. And a fight where you can actually punch instead of compliment might help you get rid of a little Angel angst.

"Ah," Giles says.

You look at him, waiting for him to go on. He keeps reading.

"Ah," he says again. "Yes. Yes." He keeps reading.

"You can't do that," you burst out. "Ah, yes, yes, *what*?"

"There have been a long line of demon queens named Belakane, in many dimensions."

"I knew it was her!" you cry. "I knew she was a jerk!"

"It seems that when a female is mature, she enters a new dimension and starts a colony of her own," Giles says.

"Colony as in . . . ant farm?" you ask.

"They share many similarities. It seems the Belakanes can take on an antlike form or a form such as our own Ms. Belakane's, or a combination of both forms," Giles explains. "She uses the inhabitants of her new world to form her new colony after evaluating their usefulness."

"The test," Willow bursts out.

"But it can't just be the test. What about the other stuff? Is it mind woo-woo?" you ask.

"It's more chemical woo-woo," Giles answers. "It seems that Ms. Belakane will have secreted a mix of pheromones that brought about the changes she desired."

"And she desired that?" You point to Xander. "Sorry, Xan."

"It's as Willow said. He is becoming one of her honeypots. The other members of Belakane's colony will feed from him and the others she has selected for that purpose," Giles says. "There's one other thing Ms. Belakane will do immediately. She will choose a mate. She will want to lay eggs and produce her first generation of offspring as quickly as possible. We need to act before that happens."

"A mate?" Willow asks. Her eyes go to you. "Buffy? Do you think . . . ?"

"What?" You're still trying to wrap your head around people eating out of Xander's stomach. How would that work?

"You said Angel was acting, um, distant. Do you think—"

"Belakane is trying to snake my boyfriend!" you cry. Relief washes over you. Angel wasn't cold and distant because he was cold and distant. And he didn't not care because he didn't care . . . or something. He's just been blasted by Belakane Number 9.

You spring to your feet. "Nobody is mating with my boyfriend but me," you announce. You feel your face get hot. "Not that I have. I mean . . . but no one else is, anyway."

"Buffy, I'm afraid there's more," Giles says. "The, er, mating process involves the draining of the mate's life force."

"And?"

"And once the life force is drained, the mate dies."

"But Angel's a vampire," you protest, your heart turning into an ice sculpture. "He doesn't have a life force. Does he?"

"I don't know what the consequence might be," Giles answers. "I've never read a case study of the union of a vampire and a demon ant queen."

One thing is clear: Belakane needs to be stopped. But if Angel is in danger, shouldn't you tell him?

"We don't know for sure that Belakane has chosen Angel as her mate," Giles says. "It's possible she's going after someone else right this instant. You have to stop her."

He's right. But . . . Angel.

What should you do?

SLAYER CHOICE:

Do you decide to . . .

❘ go warn Angel? *If yes, turn to page 210.*

❘ go kill Belakane? *If yes, turn to page 58.*

"**I** am going to kill Belakane. Right now!" You leap to your feet.

"Good," Giles says. "But I'm afraid we'll have to find her first."

"Ooh! I can do that," Willow cries. She turns to Xander. "Xander, will you take us to the colony?"

"Okay," Xander says.

You and Giles stare at her. "He's a Teddie. He's agreeable," she explains.

Xander ambles toward the door. You, Giles, and Willow follow him. And where do you end up? Where the badness so often takes place—your own Sunnydale High. More specifically, the football field. Where badness of the sporty kind also often takes place.

Cordelia and about half the cheerleading squad are spread out across the fifty yard line. They are looking kinda militant. Like they are about to protest the return of gauchos—with extreme force, if necessary. Angel is a few feet away from them. You want to run to him, but Giles puts his hand on your shoulder. "Wait a moment," he says quietly. "It's not safe."

The cheerleaders drop to their knees and paw at the grass. And it's coming right up. You realize that a hole has been dug into the football field.

Angel steps into the hole and quickly disappears from sight.

"You were correct, Buffy," Giles says. "Cordelia and the other Peppies are being used by Belakane as army ants. Angel must have gotten past them because Belakane has doused him with pheromones."

"We have to get in there. We don't know how fast Belakane's going to go after him," you say. Especially because he is wearing your favorite shirt, the midnight blue one, with the silk that feels so good under your fingers.

"What's wrong with their faces?" Willow asks, staring at the guards.

"Possibly Belakane's hormones have made some modifications to their jaws," Giles answers. "The way she, er, modified Xander's stomach."

You peer through the darkness at Cordelia's face. Yeah, her mouth is even bigger than usual.

"So if we want to get in, we have to get past Cordy and those other guards," you say.

"I imagine there are many more of them, probably hidden from sight but within easy reach of the hole," Giles tells you.

"And I can't kill them," you say. "Much as I might like to."

"No. You'd have to fight the guards, but not hurt them." Giles looks worried. "Unless there's another way into the colony."

"Does anyone have anything to eat?" Xander asks.

"Xander was zapped with the bug spray," you say. "So he can go into the colony, right?"

"Presumably," Giles says.

"You think he gets guest privileges?" you ask.

Giles rubs the bridge of his nose. "Perhaps."

"The report from the third grade said ants can

hardly see. It's all about smell in the ant kingdom," Willow volunteers.

"I don't believe their vision has been affected," Giles says. He turns to Xander, who has started eating grass. "Have you been having any trouble seeing?"

"No." Xander gives an agreeable green smile.

"We can't be certain that these mutant human ants will rely solely on scent to determine whether to allow entrance into the colony," Giles says.

"Do we have any other choice?" you ask.

"Well, we can look for a back door," Giles suggests. "That would be the prudent move."

But Belakane's been screwing with half the school— and your boyfriend. You don't feel like being prudent.

What do you do?

SLAYER CHOICE:

Do you decide to . . .

❘ try to use Xander to get you into the colony?
If yes, turn to page 61.

❘ try to find a different entrance to the colony?
If yes, turn to page 227.

"We have to risk it." You grab Xander by the arm. "Come on, we're going in. Stay really close to us so all they smell is you."

"Okay," Xander says.

"I'm not certain this is the best idea," Giles says as he, Willow, and you head toward the fifty yard line clustered around Xander.

"What do we do if they don't like the way we smell?" Willow asks, glancing over at the mutant Peppies.

"You run, and I kick and punch," you say. "But with the diffuser on. I don't want to really hurt any of them. Just make them go sleepy-bye for a little while."

"But how can you fight them all without hurting anyone?" Willow asks.

"I guess I'll just have to . . . improvise," you say.

Cordelia turns her head toward your little group. So do the other guards. But they don't make a move toward you. So you keep moving toward the entrance to the colony. Closer, closer, closer.

"Xander Harris, party of four," you say.

Cordy and company stay where they are. You reach the hole and see stairs dug into the ground inside it. You nudge Willow, and she climbs in first. Then Giles. Then Xander. Then you, staying as close to Xander—and his smell—as you can.

The plan worked. You're in Belakane's colony.

You climb down the steps that have been carved into the earth. At the bottom, you reach a narrow tunnel that's high enough for you to stand in without stooping. "Run!" you yell. "We have to get to Angel!"

Xander's stomach slurps and sloshes as you race down the tunnel. "Wait!" he cries when the tunnel widens into a room. He stops and heads over to Matt Lopez, who is working to make the room larger by digging out one of the walls—with his humongazoid, clawlike hands.

"Hey, Matt. Want some cookies?" Xander asks.

"Yeah," Matt says.

"One sec." Xander's translucent belly heaves and rolls. Then he pukes into his hands.

"Oh, good god," Giles mutters.

Bile burns your throat, and you turn your head away, but not before you see Xander transfer the orange-and-green mess into Matt's hands.

"Come on, we've got to keep moving," you say. Xander will just have to catch up to you when he's done . . . feeding people.

You imagine yourself in one of those plastic-sided ant farms as you and the others travel deeper into the earth. You pass more kids from school, working away. No one asks where you're going or what you're doing there. They're digging furiously, as if digging is the new dancing.

You realize that the tunnel you're in is getting wider. And lighter. There is a little runway of light going on made of battery-powered glowing discs.

Brian Williams from the Debate Club steps in front of you, followed by Jin Park from the Future Home-makers.

"Stop right there," Brian says. His jaw drops down—

way down. Practically to his chest. His teeth lengthen into black fangs, complete with little barbs on the sides.

Giles punches him. "Go, Buffy!" he yells. "Get Belakane!"

Willow kicks Jin in the shin.

· You hope they'll be okay. You sprint down the runway of little lights. They lead into a swanky lounge with a sofa–love seat combo—

And an Angel-Belakane combo.

They're sitting together on the sofa. She's practically in his lap. Her big dark saucer eyes are staring up at Angel. Her lips are inches away from his. Parted. Ready for big-time smoochies.

With *your* boyfriend.

SLAYER ACTION:
Turn to page 64.

"Angel, no!" you scream. You dash over and shove Belakane away from him. "She's an ant demon. She's poisoned your mind."

He stares at you like he's never seen you before. You do the only thing you can. You punch him in the jaw as hard as you can. Pain rockets up your arm. You ignore it, and punch him again. "You love me," you tell him.

"He loves me," Belakane corrects. Her words come out distorted because her jaws are now huge, and as sharp and jagged as a saw blade. She tosses her head, her long black hair spilling down her back. Then she curves one finger at Angel. "Come here," she orders.

He takes a step toward her. "Angel! Stay away from her," you cry. You execute a snap-kick to his chest. His face vamps out. Uh-oh. He takes another step toward Belakane.

He doesn't seem to care that Belakane's body is changing. Her dark eyes widen . . . literally. The eyes grow farther apart as her nose moves forward, turning a dark brown color. Antennae shoot straight up from her head. Her arms lengthen, becoming segmented black legs. Her abdomen extends into a huge, swollen poison sac with a stinger on one end.

You stare at her. The sleek woman in the suit is gone. Belakane is a humongous black ant.

"Angel, look at her!" you shout. You hurl yourself between the two of them. You spin and do a round-house kick to Belakane's throat, then continue around and land another kick to Angel's chest. "She's evil. She's what we fight! Together!"

You've become a Buffy sandwich between Angel and Belakane. They're moving in tight. Belakane drops her jaws open wide. You feel the blades of her maw slide around the sides of your head. You slam your elbows back into her abdomen. Angel grabs you by the wrists—

And pulls you free.

"Angel?" Belakane cries, bewildered.

He answers by snapping her neck. Then he turns and looks at you, really looks at you.

"You're back."

He answers by kissing you. And kissing you. And kissing you.

"This is making me want to hurl," Xander says.

You break away from the kissing long enough to look up. Willow, Giles, and Xander are all watching you. Behind them, a bunch of baffled-looking kids from school are wandering around the dirt hallway. Their mouths are all normal, and Xander's enormous stomach has disappeared.

There's going to be a lot of "explaining" to do once you all get back up to the surface. But for now, you kiss Angel just one more time.

You've earned it.

THE END

10. You're a mouse. A kitten stands between you and a piece of cheese big enough to feed your whole family. What do you do?

I fire whoever made up this kindergarten-on-drugs test, you think. So far, every question on the Be the Ultimate You! test has been more mind-numbingly ridiculous than the one before. And you have twenty more to go. How are questions about mice and crayons and blades of grass really going to help you build self-esteem? And how are you ever going to explain to Giles why you had to be here taking this stupid test rather than with him, training?

You chew on the end of your number-two pencil and study the multiple-choice answers to the question:

A. run and hide

B. make a dash for the cheese and hope the kitten doesn't catch you

C. wait until the kitten leaves

Kick the kitten's butt in hand-to-hand combat, you think. That's what you'd do if some mangy cat tried to keep you away from cheese. Your stomach rumbles as you let yourself picture a nice plate of Brie for a minute—no time for breakfast this a.m. With a sigh, you fill in the circle next to answer B. That's the problem with standardized tests. They never have the answer you'd actually give, and so you end up choosing one that isn't exactly like you. And then the results are wonky, but you're supposed to treat them as gospel truth anyway. You still haven't stopped taking the love quizzes in *Cosmopolitan,* though, because hope springs eternal. Besides, the alternative to bad multiple-choice is a test full of essays, and you wouldn't wish that on your worst enemy. Well, *maybe* on your worst enemy. It would be nice to see Spike or the Master be forced to take an all-essay test.

11. There is one lollipop left in the jar. Your sister wants it. So do you. What do you do?

Once again, I choose butt-kicking, you think. You take a moment to thank the powers that be that you don't have a sister, lollipop-hogging or otherwise. Life as an only child suits you fine—and that's the way it will always be.

A. take the lollipop for yourself
B. give the lollipop to your sister
C. split the lollipop

Split the lollipop? What kind of reality-defying answer is that? You can't split a lollipop. You can't even share one, unless maybe with your boyfriend. You wonder if Angel likes lollipops, and indulge yourself in a little sweet-sharing fantasy until Xander shifts in the seat next to you, startling you out of the pleasantness.

You fill in the circle next to A.

12. You must choose from three entrées at a restaurant. Which do you choose?

There goes the stomach rumbling again. It's so unfair to make you take a test during lunch. And it's downright sadistic to put all these food-type questions on the test. You study the answers, wishing the test were a menu.

A. cat food

B. lettuce

C. sugar

And you're stumped. What kind of freaky restaurant serves cat food? Not to mention lettuce or sugar. As a garnish, sure. As an additive to your coffee, definitely. But as an entrée? You stare at the choices, willing them to make sense. But the Force isn't working for you today. It's a bizarre question, with bizarre answers. You glance over at Xander's paper to see what he's done with this one. But he's still on question five. Should you ask for help? It seems kind of lame. Maybe you should just pick one and move on. But then, maybe there's a catch.

You get up and head toward the front of the room. Ms. Belakane and her fabulous boots are sitting at a table up near the cafeteria doors. You'll just double-check with her. Who knows? Maybe you got a test form with some weird typo on it.

Your fabulous boots, they are clompy. In the quiet lunchroom your footsteps sound like the hooves of a Clydesdale, and you're worried that everyone will be annoyed. So you do what any normal person would do while creating a ruckus in a silent exam room—walk faster and keep your head down to avoid any eye contact with pissed-off classmates. Except in this case . . . yuck.

Ants. Creepy, crawly, ugly, industrious little ants. Winding their way along the linoleum floor of the caf. At first it's just a few stragglers. Little ants walking in circles, or tracing some sort of serpentine line along the floor in search of a few fallen crumbs. Then two or three ants together, walking with purpose.

And as you continue walking toward the front? More ants. In lines. Definite, straight, well-defined lines. Three or four or five ants across, marching together toward the cafeteria doors. It's kind of mesmerizing. You watch the ants as you walk, forgetting to worry about your loud shoes and the bizarre test question. You've never seen ants acting in such harmony, as if someone has put up the directions to an ant rave on the ant Internet and now they're all heading straight there . . . to Ms. Belakane.

You look up, surprised. You'd been so busy staring at the creepy crawlies that you hadn't been paying attention to where you were. But here was the table at the front, and here was Ms. Belakane, a binder full of student transcripts open before her. She looks at you with her huge dark eyes.

"Can I help you?" Her voice is deep and gravelly. Her suit jacket is seriously gorgeous. But you can't get your mind off the ants. Where are they?

"Um . . . yeah," you mutter, staring down at the floor. The line of ants disappears under the table. You stand on tiptoes to look over Ms. Belakane's head. Behind her, the floor is clear. No crawling lines. So where were they all marching to?

"Did you have a question?" Ms. Belakane prompts you.

"I have a confusion," you say. "About a question. Or about the answers." You realize you're sort of babbling, but you just have to know where the insects are. How can you feel comfortable in your chair if you know there are thousands of ants crawling around the room and vanishing? You reach out and knock the student binder off the table. "Oh!" you gasp. "I'm so sorry! I'm such a klutz." Fast as lightning, you kneel and peer under the table.

The line of ants is there, winding across the floor and up the legs of Ms. Belakane's chair.

"Oh, my god," you shriek. You jump back up, snatching the binder from the floor before the ants incorporate it into their line. "There are ants all over you!"

Ms. Belakane stares at you blankly. "Excuse me?"

"Ants!" you cry. How can she not get it? Aren't they crawling on her legs? "Ants," you add helpfully.

She just blinks those big eyes. "I'm afraid I don't understand."

But as she reaches for the student binder, you spot a tiny ant crawling along her hand. "Look!" You reach out to squish it. "They're everywhere."

"Stop!" Ms. Belakane yells.

You stop, finger poised half an inch above the little bug.

"I can't believe you were going to kill him. He's done nothing to you!" Ms. Belakane shoots you an angry look as she grabs a piece of paper and holds it to her hand until the ant crawls off onto the paper. She leans down to let the ant off the paper onto the floor. It walks off, and you know it's just going to rejoin the line of ants already there. You stare at Ms. Belakane. Are the ants all over her? But you don't see any more of them.

"Sorry," you say. "I was just trying to help."

"By murdering an innocent creature?" she demands. She's talking loudly now, and you're probably attracting even more attention than you did with your boots.

"Sorry," you mumble.

Her expression softens a bit. "All right. So Miss . . . Summers, is it?" she asks. "Did you need something?"

You stare at her in her posh clothes with her sleek black hair and dark eyes. She's an education tester, you remind yourself. So what if she has a soft spot for ants? There's nothing criminal about that.

But what about the trail of ants?

There must be a hole in the linoleum under her chair, you realize. *The ants are going in there and heading underground.*

Right?

Ms. Belakane was a little hyper about the ant-squishing. That's odd, but not supernatural. And ants in a line? So annoyingly natural. So what should you do?

SLAYER CHOICE:

Do you decide to . . .

\ ask for help on the question, then finish the test? So what if this lady has a bug fetish? *If yes, turn to page 87.*

\ say you're not feeling well and ask to be excused? Something's weird about this chick. *If yes, turn to page 72.*

"I . . . uh . . . I don't feel well," you lie. What you really want to say is, *I need to get away from these weird swarming ants, and a little distance from you wouldn't hurt either, ant-loving lady*. You suck your cheeks in a little, hoping it makes you look gaunt.

"You're sick?" she asks, as if that's surprising. She's clearly not used to dealing with the high school set. Any experienced teacher would already have the suspicious face on.

"I'm feeling a little faint," you say. And that's not entirely a lie. Not eating all day, combined with thousands of ants that might be crawling on your feet this very second, *has* made you a wee bit queasy. "I think I need to go to the nurse."

"Oh." Ms. Belakane looks helpless. "Um . . . okay."

"I need a hall pass," you tell her.

Now she looks even more overwhelmed. You take pity on her, pull a slip of paper from the binder, and write "Pass" and "Buffy Summers" on it. You slide it across the desk to Ms. Belakane.

"What do I have to do?" she asks.

"Just give me your autograph," you chirp. Then she does get the suspicious face, and you remember you're supposed to be sick. You suck your cheeks back in and attempt to look pathetic.

Ms. Belakane signs the pass, and you get out of there as fast as you can. The ants are still there, swarming up the floor to her table. It's hard to believe nobody else has noticed, but that's Sunnydale High for you. You stop long enough to grab your bag and give Xander a smile, then you're free.

Out into the hallway, down the stairs at the end, and a left. You're at the library before you even know it. The feeling of ants crawling on you begins to subside the instant you step through the door. The library is safe. It's almost as much of a haven of sanity as your very own bedroom. And Giles is here. He'll figure out the deal with the ants. He's good with the figuring out.

"You're late," Giles says. "Where's Willow?"

"She's still taking the test. Snyder personally dragged us there. But not the point. You've got to help," you cry. "There's an anthill in the cafeteria."

He barely even glances up from his dusty old tome. "That's not surprising," he murmurs. "I don't believe that place has been mopped one single time since I've been working here."

"No, I mean there's something weird. Crawling, swarming, antenna—" You break off. "Antennae-ed? Antenna-ish? Anyway, it's weird with a capital *W*. And antennae."

Now Giles does look up, giving you his patented why-must-American-teenagers-be-so-foolish grimace. "I'm sorry?" he asks politely.

"Ants," you say. "Lots and lots of ants."

Giles blinks. "Are they giant?"

"Uh, no."

"Are they mutants?"

"No . . ."

"Are they in any way supernatural?"

You're forced to admit they are not. "They're gross, though," you assure him. "And they seem to really like Ms. Belakane."

"My ears must be ringing," says a deep voice from the doorway. You spin around, and there she is. Ms. Belakane, with her pointy-toed boots and her big brown eyes . . . and you are so busted. You don't know which to be embarrassed about first: the fact that she caught you in the library when you're supposed to be at the nurse, or the fact that she caught you talking about *her*.

You think fast. And come up with nothing. "Um . . . ," you say.

"Miss Summers. I assume you're feeling better?" she asks.

"Are you ill, Buffy?" asks Sir Giles the Clueless.

"Yes," you tell him through clenched teeth. "I am sick and that is why I had to leave Ms. Belakane's test early."

"Oh." He frowns as he thinks that through. "Oh!"

"I thought you were going to the nurse," Ms. Belakane says.

"So you followed me?" you reply. Sometimes a good offense is the best confuser of adults seeking to yell.

"Yes. I was concerned. You were *very* pale." Her voice trembles ever so slightly, and her big eyes are filled with hurt because you lied to her. She's good. She's very, very good. You may well have met your match. And that means getting sent to Principal Snyder, and detention, and maternal disapproval. You have to find a way out of this.

"I just needed to pick up . . . something . . . before heading to the nurse," you say. "Because I figured she'd send me home, and so I needed my . . . something . . . before I left."

"Here it is!" Giles cries happily. He shoves a dusty copy of *Around the World in Eighty Days* into your hands.

You stare at him. This is supposed to be helpful? But miraculously, it works.

"I love that book," Ms. Belakane says.

"You do?" you ask doubtfully.

"Yes, well, Buffy is reading it for extra credit," Giles tells her. "She's always trying to get in some reading time, even when she feels a bit under the weather."

"That's very commendable." Ms. Belakane smiles at you. "I'm terribly sorry that you're going to miss the rest of the Be the Ultimate You! test."

"Me too," you say. "But I feel kinda stomach flu-ey and then all those ants pushed me over the edge."

"Ants . . . ," Giles says slowly. Finally he's beginning to get the whole picture.

"There were a lot of ants in the cafeteria, and Buffy was upset by them," Ms. Belakane tells him. "I don't know why they'd cause such a reaction. I myself am fascinated by the entire species."

"They are quite an interesting species," Giles agrees. "I recently saw a documentary on fire ant colonies in southern Peru. It was truly an eye-opening experience."

As is this. Your eyes are being opened to the fact that Giles is even more of a nerd than you thought.

"Peru?" Ms. Belakane beams at him. "I assume it involved the Dinoponera?"

"Yes, in fact, it did." Giles gazes at her as if she were one of his beloved books of demonology. He's smitten. It's horrifying to watch. "Are you familiar with—"

"I gotta go," you interrupt. "You know, because I'm nauseous. And the ants made it worse. So the ant talk? Not helping."

"They're really quite harmless," Giles tells you.

"Well, except for the fire ants and the bull ants and the driver ants," Ms. Belakane puts in, laying a perfectly manicured hand on Giles's arm.

He laughs loudly. "Of course, yes, except for those!"

"Yeah, so . . . enough with the ants," you reiterate.

"You shouldn't underestimate them, Buffy," Ms. Belakane says. "Ants have quite highly evolved civilizations."

"In fact, ants were already farming—expertly—before Homo sapiens even diverged from the chimpanzee," Giles backs her up.

"Oh," you say. They're not paying attention to you anymore, anyway. They can't take their eyes off each other. Giles is actually leaning toward Ms. Belakane, as if they're talking about their undying love for each other and not about ants.

"You know," she purrs, holding out her hand, "we

haven't been introduced. My name is Victoria."

Giles takes her hand and holds it. Not even pretending to shake.

"I'm sorry," you say loudly. "This is Mr. Giles. The *librarian*." That should be enough to scare any normal woman away. But Ms. Belakane just gives a slow smile.

"Wonderful," she murmurs.

"Call me Rupert," Giles says.

"Rupert." She makes it sound like a term of endearment or something. You're getting that skin-crawly feeling again, only this time it has nothing to do with ants. You back toward the door. This adult flirtatiousness is creeping you out.

"There's a band playing at a nightclub tonight," Ms. Belakane says. You stop in your tracks. That was an abrupt subject change. "Several of the students are in it. I thought I might swing by. I like to show the teenagers that adults can be a part of their lives—that we take an interest in them. Like you obviously do with Buffy."

Giles blushes and smiles coyly. You can barely stand it.

"I find it helps them learn to love themselves a bit more," Ms. Belakane continues. "If teens don't feel so alone in the world, their self-esteem skyrockets."

"I wholeheartedly agree," Giles tells her. "So many educators treat the students as lesser beings. It must wreak havoc with their self-esteem."

Okay, now you've had enough. Giles sounds like a

self-help book. Wasn't he supposed to be opposed to Ms. Belakane's category-intensive program?

"Maybe you'd like to come with me," Ms. Belakane purrs. "The band is playing at a place called the Bronze."

"I'd love to," Giles answers immediately.

Ah. Hence the self-esteem psychobabble. It was all an elaborate ruse to make a date. You're willing to forgive that.

"Shall we meet there?" Ms. Belakane asks.

"Why don't we have dinner beforehand?" Giles suggests.

"That would be wonderful, but I'm afraid I can't. I'll be at the school until six, meeting with students to go over their Ultimate You! test results," Ms. Belakane tells him.

"Are you meeting with the students individually?" Giles asks. "That's very thorough."

"I'm a very thorough lady."

You imagine her thoroughness is gonna piss a lot of people off. Nobody mentioned having to do after-school meetings in order to Be the Ultimate You!

"I'll meet you at the Bronze, then," Giles says.

"See you there," Ms. Belakane practically growls in her gravelly voice. She leaves without a glance at you. Finally you can smack some sense into Giles.

"Giles! You have a date with Ms. Calendar later," you cry. "Are you planning to cut short your coffee date with her in order to meet Miss Self-Esteem at the Bronze?"

He looks at you blankly.

"Date," you repeat. "Jenny Calendar."

"Hmm. I guess I'll have to cancel that." He heads off into his office, leaving you behind. Shocked. What's happened to Giles?

SLAYER ACTION:
Turn to page 80.

You're still staring at Giles's retreating back as Willow and Xander come through the doors.

"Buffy! What happened?" Willow cries.

"Yeah, we saw the self-esteem-or-die lady on her way out," Xander adds. "Did she follow you?"

"Are you suspended?" Willow asks.

"No." You're kinda shocked by lack of lie-to-test-lady-skip-test-go-to-library punishment yourself, now that you think about it. "She just flirted with Giles and left."

Two pairs of confused eyes gaze back at you. "Come again?" Xander says.

"They . . . they *flirted*," you say, still reeling from the memory. "By talking about ants. And self-esteem."

"Ants?" Willow sounds confused.

"And then they made a date," you continue.

"What? Giles is going out with Queen Freaky?" Xander shakes his head. "That's not right. She's all touchy-feely—"

"But in a totalitarian sort of way," Willow puts in.

"Right, with the test taking and the categorizing and the witch boots," Xander agrees. You hide your own pointy-toed boots by stepping behind one of the library counters. Xander doesn't notice—he's still ranting. "And Giles is . . . well, he's—"

"He's Giles," Willow finishes for him. "He's kinda cool. You know, following the so-uncool-it-hurts methodology."

"Exactly," you say. "He was totally against the

Ultimate You! test. And yet he's going to the Bronze with Ms. Belakane."

Utter silence. Willow's brow is furrowed in confusion. Xander frowns.

"The Bronze?" Xander finally says. "Giles is going on a date to a high school hangout?"

"I've never had a date at the Bronze," Willow says. "Why does Giles get to have a date at our date place before I do? That's unfair! He should get his own date place!"

"Apparently there's a band playing there tonight," you tell them. "Ms. Belakane wants to support them. It will help their self-esteem."

"Yes. Because musicians have such low self-worth, what with all the groupies and the band glow," Xander says sarcastically.

"Band glow?" you ask.

"The mysterious phenomenon that causes even the scrawniest, greasiest guy on the planet to become a sex god the instant he straps on a guitar," Xander defines it for you.

"Oh." You nod. "Band glow."

"Wait a minute!" Willow practically shrieks. "At the Bronze? Tonight? Oz! The Dingoes."

You shoot Xander a questioning look. He shrugs.

"Huh?" you ask.

"It's Oz. It's his band. Dingoes Ate My Baby."

You think back to this morning, that beautiful time before the weirdness that was Giles and Ms. Belakane. Willow asked about a guy who was always looking at her. "Oz is in a band?"

"Yes. Dingoes Ate My—"

"Well, then, we should go," you interrupt Willow. "*You* should go. It will totally get his attention."

All the blood drains from Willow's face. "I don't want his attention."

"Yes, you do."

"No. I mean, yes. But no." Willow sinks into a wooden library chair.

"Will, he likes you," you point out. "You like him. You should go to his gig to show him that you like him."

"But what if he sees me there?" Willow whispers.

"Then our evil plan will have worked," you tell her.

"Pardon me for intruding on this special moment," Xander says. "But isn't Giles going to be at the Bronze? Dating? On a date? Daterizing?"

He has a point. You bite your lip for a moment, imagining the dating behavior of a mature British nerd. It's not something you really want to see up close and personal. On the other hand, it's a prime opportunity to get Willow out into the Romantic World Beyond Xander Harris. What should you do?

SLAYER CHOICE:

Do you decide to . . .

\ go to the Bronze? *If yes, turn to page 17.*

\ blow off the Bronze and go patrolling? The risk of permanent psychological damage from witnessing Giles's date is too great. *If yes, turn to page 83.*

"**I** mean, ewww, right?" you ask Angel. You kick your heels against the gravestone you're sitting on as you tell him the tale of Giles and She Who Likes Ants. "Would you really want to kiss someone who gets off on bugs?"

"Maybe he's not planning to kiss her," Angel says. He leans in for a kiss of his own, but you're distracted. You've been patrolling for an hour—well, hanging with Angel for half an hour and patrolling for the half hour before that. But you still can't get the image of flirty Giles out of your head.

"How can he do this to Miss Calendar?" you ask. "He completely blew her off for this chick he just met. That doesn't sound like Giles, does it?"

Angel runs his hand through his hair. "No." He's frustrated, you can tell. He wants to be making out. And normally you'd want that too. You need to shake off the worry and pay attention to what matters: your gorgeous, sweet, and undead boyfriend. You take his hand and hop down from the gravestone. "Let's take a walk," you suggest.

He strolls along next to you, the two of you picking your way through the cemetery. "You're worried about Giles," Angel says.

"I guess I am," you admit. "He just wasn't acting like himself."

"But you've never seen him when he's dating someone," Angel pointed out. "Maybe this is how he acts."

"All inconsiderate and rude to Jenny Calendar?"

"It's possible," Angel says. "He met this Ms. Belakane, he was attracted to her, and he acted on it. It's not like he and Ms. Calendar are a couple or anything."

"You're right." He's right. You know he's right. You try to ignore your concern for Giles and turn to look up at your boyfriend. "You wouldn't do that, would you? Meet somebody new and drop me with no warning?"

"No." He stops walking and pulls you into his arms. "Because I'm in love with you. It's a completely different situation." He kisses you, and all your worry melts away. You're lost in the beauty that is Angel.

Light falls across your faces, blindingly bright. You ignore it and keep kissing Angel. But when the odd cracking, snapping, whooshing sound comes, you know you have to check it out. You pull away from Angel and glance over at the light. It's white and pulsing and generally otherworldish. Which means bad. The otherworldish is never good. And the sound keeps coming . . . right up until the giant golden slide appears. As soon as the bottom of the slide hits the ground, the whooshing sound stops. You glance at Angel.

"Is that a . . . playground slide?" he asks.

"For a giant," you reply.

And then, unfortunately, the giant appears. He's eight feet tall, with orangey-red hair and rosy cheeks. He's dressed entirely in a green velvet suit—top hat and everything. He swoops down the golden slide straight toward you, and you get the strangest sense of déjà vu. "Oh, my god, it's the leprechaun from my dream!" you cry.

"There are no such things as leprechauns," Angel replies. "That's a Sleaninhnam demon."

You roll your eyes. "You say tomato—"

"Duck!" Angel snaps. You crouch down just as a humongous black mallet whizzes through the air right where your head was a split second ago. Angel punches the green giant in the chest. The Sleaninhnam demon barely budges.

"The chest?" you ask.

"It's as high as I can reach," Angel retorts. "He's really tall."

The mallet whizzes by again. You both jump out of the way, and you take the opportunity to get a good look at the Sleaninhnam demon. Like the Lucky Charms guy on serious steroids—until he turns his twinkly blue eyes on you. And they are indeed twinkling—with pure hatred. His chubby face twists in a snarl, and he swings the giant mallet again.

"How do I kill him when I can't even reach him?" you ask.

Angel's expression is grim. "I don't know how to kill them. I'm not sure they're killable. Didn't Giles tell you?"

The mallet swings again, catching you in the side. It hurts like nothing you've ever felt. What is that thing made of? You fall to the ground, trying to get your breath. Angel is still fighting, but that demon is stronger than both of you. It's a losing battle.

You try to remember what Giles said about the Sleaninhnam demon, but all you can recall is that he wanted to tell you more. He wanted a special training session . . . and then he got all caught up in Ms. Belakane.

He didn't tell you what you need to know.

"Buffy, look out!"

You roll painfully to your side—just in time to see the mallet speeding toward your head.

And then blackness.

THE END

"**T**he question about what to order at the restaurant, it started making my head hurt," you confess to Ms. Belakane. "Although maybe it was just hunger pains. Because of missing lunch. Is it some kind of trick, maybe?" You lower your voice. "Are people with good self-esteem supposed to refuse to keep taking the test at some point?"

Now that you say that out loud, it seems like the most obvious thing in the world. Hey, maybe you have the highest self-esteem in the room, because you started thinking the test was too nutsy for school before anyone else.

"Because, cat food or a plate of sugar?" you rush on. "Not going to happen at even a really bad half-a-star kind of place."

Ms. Belakane smiles. "You're thinking too much."

"Oh." So much for your brilliant I'm-too-emotionally-healthy-to-take-this-test idea.

"What I want you to do is read the question and mark the answer that you're most drawn to," Ms. Belakane says. "I'm interested in your instincts. Forget about logic. Just have fun with it."

Fun test. Is she insane? Fun and test are not peanut butter and jelly. Or even peanut butter and chocolate. You tell yourself not to make any sudden movements. Ms. Belakane is clearly a little . . . off. "Okay, I'll try."

"The point is not to try," Ms. Belakane says.

"Okay. No thinking and no trying," you say.

"Right."

You head back to your seat. *Don't think or try,* you tell yourself. You should be able to handle that.

SLAYER ACTION:
Turn to page 89.

"**I** feel violated," Xander complains as you meet up after school. "I feel like Ms. Belakane has been poking around in my brain with her long, creepy fingers. Do you think I have enough for a lawsuit that will bring me in mounds of dough so I can quit school and live the life of decadence that I am so highly suited for?"

"Where you can go out to fine restaurants and dine on the best cat food every night?" you joke.

"What was with those questions?" Xander asks. "The one about the jack-in-the-box and the unicorn? No normal brain could come up with that. I'm telling you, there is something deeply wrong with Ms. Belakane. She may have been one of those kids raised in a basement or something."

"My theory? Not a self-esteem thingie at all. The test is a new way to screen for drug use," you say. "But if taking it and having a little meeting with Ms. Let's-All-Feel-Super-Good-About-Ourselves keeps the Snyder monkey off my back, I'm a happy Buffy."

"You guys!" Willow comes rushing up. "We need to get to the library."

"On our way," you tell her.

"Giles was *not* happy that you didn't train at lunchtime, Buffy," Willow says.

You sigh. There's just no way to make everyone happy. "But I sent you instead," you point out. "You're the next best thing to me. You're even better than me, research-wise."

Willow's face breaks out into a proud smile. "You should've seen me," she tells Xander. "When Principal

Snyder was all in Buffy's face about taking the test, I just faked sick and he totally let me go!"

"And that's good why?" Xander asks.

"Because I couldn't get out of the test," you explain. "I figured at least Will could go start with the research so we'll have *some* prep if the green demon shows."

You push open the big swinging doors to the library and are met with the musty old book smell.

"Good, you're here," Giles says. "We have to leave immediately. The Sleaninhnam demon has been spotted on State Street, near the cinema."

"Um, I'm supposed to be at my self-esteem session with Ms. Belakane in"—you check your sassy Supergirl watch—"twenty minutes. Principal Snyder was very principally about me going."

Giles stares at you as if he wants to you find him more threatening than Snyder. Not gonna happen. Snyder wins on threatening.

But Giles wins on doing the right thing. You're the Slayer. You're supposed to go fight the demon.

Still, detention looms if you skip your Ms. Belakane session. What's a girl to do?

SLAYER CHOICE:
Do you decide to . . .

\ go see about the green demon? *If yes, turn to page 91.*

\ go to your meeting with Ms. Belakane? *If yes, turn to page 94.*

"**S**orry," you say to Giles. "It's just hard for me to think of a leprechaun as a big threat to the world as we know it. Even a giant leprechaun." You clap your hands. "Let's move, people. We don't want anyone to get damaged by a shamrock."

"The Sleaninhnam is not a leprechaun," Giles says, and his voice has that strained tone that it gets when he has repeated himself a coupleish times. "You must have realized that from your dreams."

"Well, he had a green suit, and rosy cheeks, and a top hat—also green," you protest as your group of fearless baddie fighters heads out to the parking lot. "Can you think of anybody besides a leprechaun who fits that description?"

"A baby dressed up as a leprechaun for Halloween?" Xander offers.

"Or, oooh, a clown whose favorite color is green," Willow suggests. "But his suit would need one of those squirty flowers on the lapel."

Giles doesn't bother answering. He just unlocks his car, and you all cram inside. And you do mean cram. His car isn't that much bigger than a toy. In fact, it's about the right size for a leprechaun—a non-jumbo Sleaninhnam one—but you don't say that, because you can tell Giles is not finding the talk of the little people in green all that amusing. And when Giles isn't amused, you've discovered that you end up having training sessions that leave you needing ice packs for your ouching muscles.

"I wish I'd been able to find out more about the

demon when I was researching during lunch. I was going to do more after school, but after school, we heard he was out, so no time," Willow says as Giles pulls out of the parking lot and heads toward State Street. "I know he uses a mallet in his battles."

"Mallet. Check," you say.

"And he's about eight feet tall, and weighs approximately four hundred pounds," Willow continues.

"Check. And check," you say. But your throat is feeling a little dry. And you're wishing your boots had higher heels. Even though your piggies would be squealing at the top of their lungs. Not that your toes actually have lungs. Or that they are actually piggies, for that matter.

"Is the demon still sounding quite so much like a leprechaun?" Giles enquires.

You want to smack him. But he's your Watcher. That wouldn't be respectful. And you'd be in huge trouble. And he might not help you with the eight-foot, four-hundred-pound, rosy-cheeked leprechaun. Yes, leprechaun!

Giles rounds the corner. And you see it. The demon.

It's tall, all right. Over eight feet. But it doesn't weigh any four hundred pounds. It can't even crack one fifty. Not with those skinny legs. They look like stilts.

In fact, they *are* stilts. Stilts inside long green pants.

"Hey! He's not a real leprechaun," Xander exclaims.

"For the last time, there *are* no real leprechauns," Giles insists.

"He is very tall, though," Willow comments. "And I think his red hair is real."

You roll down the window. "Impersonate a Sl— Sl—a leprechaun demon, and I impersonate kicking your butt," you call up to the college-age guy in the suit.

"Huh?" He cups his hand behind his ear and leans forward. He begins to wobble on his stilts, back and forth, back and forth, and a second later he's down on the sidewalk. His face turns red under his painted-on rosy cheeks. "Uh, you want to try the new green coffee at the Espresso Pump?" he mumbles. "I got coupons."

"No," Giles replies. "No, thank you."

"Can we get back to school so I can have my happy-to-be-Buffy meeting with Ms. Belakane?" you ask as Giles pulls away from the curb again. "If I miss it, you all have to say something nice to me every day for a month."

SLAYER ACTION:
Turn to page 94.

You step into Ms. Belakane's office for your very special meeting and get a surprise of the unpleasant kind. Principal Snyder is sitting next to her. And he looks very pleased with himself. The only time Principal Snyder looks pleased with himself is when he has an occasion to make someone else feel bad. He's the one who is in dire need of a self-esteem coach, if anyone wants your opinion. Not that school is a place where anyone seems to want your opinion the majority of the time.

"Buffy, welcome," Ms. Belakane says in her deep, gravelly voice. "Come sit with us."

You sit. You wonder what the test said about you that has made Principal Snyder so very happy. Then you remind yourself of the kind of cat-food-and-lollipop-loving questions that were on Ms. Belakane's exam. If the test said something horrible about you, that would be good, because the test came from Loco Town. "So what's the verdict?" you joke. Well, you meant for it to be a joke, but it didn't come out sounding jokey. You actually sounded a little nervousey, and that made Principal Snyder smile. Toad.

"You came out as a Peppie—99.3 percent," Ms. Belakane answers. "It's very unusual for one person to show so strongly in a single category."

"Oh," you say. Are you supposed to know what to do with that information? "Um . . . what's a Peppie?"

"A Peppie is someone whose strongest character trait is aggression," Ms. Belakane says.

"The majority of people who would be 90 percent

Peppie or above on Ms. Belakane's scale are in prison," Snyder jumps in. "Or they've already been executed by the state if they live in a state that allows the death penalty." He sits back in his seat, beaming. That is so why he came to this meeting. He had to tell you that himself. Evil toad man.

"Don't worry too much, Miss Summers," Principal Snyder adds. "I've heard that lethal injection is relatively painless."

Ms. Belakane shoots him a severe look. She really does have a dominatrix vibe going. "It's true that aggression is a Peppie's main strength," she tells you. "But aggression doesn't have to be used in a way that is detrimental to society. I'm sure General Patton was a Peppie. And Mike Tyson. And Martha Stewart." She reaches out and pats your hand.

"Also Jeffrey Dahmer," Principal Snyder mutters.

Warmth spreads through your body. Warmth and happiness. She's right. There's nothing wrong with being aggressive, not if you use it for the good of society. Which you *totally* do. You feel proud to be a Peppie, at one with Patton, Mike, Martha, and Jeffrey. You can actually feel your self-esteem improving.

And it's all thanks to Ms. Belakane. You wish you could do something for her as a thank-you. A card. Or some chocolate. Or maybe she needs a bodyguard. You could do that! That would be using your aggression in a positive way.

"Just remember, the more of a Peppie you are, the more power you have to achieve," Ms. Belakane says.

"Nothing can stop you, Buffy. Nothing can get by you. You are destined for greatness."

You reach out both hands for hers. You just want to touch her one more time. Yes, you get the warm again. Like a bubble bath on the inside. In one short meeting, Ms. Belakane has inspired you so much. She has completely changed your life! "You're the best," you tell her, then you reluctantly leave the room. Principal Snyder follows you and heads into his own office.

You see Xander walking down the hall toward you. "My turn with Ms. B-b-b"—Xander flips his bottom lip with his finger in the universal gesture for lost it— "Belakane."

A bolt of angry heat rips through you. "Don't," you order.

"Don't what?" Xander asks.

"Don't mock," you say. Your heart rate has sped up, and you feel your nostrils flare.

"That's like saying don't breathe," Xander answers.

"I love her," you explain.

Xander laughs. "I get it. You're mocking while telling me not to mock. Nice." He saunters into Ms. Belakane's office with a little wave.

You start toward the library to train with Giles, walking on fluffy clouds of self-esteem. You have never liked yourself more. You even seem to smell better.

"Hey, Buffy, you have your meeting with Ms. Belakane?" Oz asks from his seat on the wooden bench next to one of the many trophy cases around the school.

"Uh-huh." You stop, muscles tense, and wait to see what he has to say about her.

"Me too. I really loved her." Oz gives a slow couple nods, like he's listening to a great tune in his head.

"Yeah," you answer.

"What'd you turn out to be?" he asks, staring down at his hands.

"A Peppie. I'm all aggressive, but in a good, non-scary way," you answer. "You?"

"I'm a Mommie. Which means I'm a nurturing kind of person. I never thought about myself that way. But when I look at this picture of my cousin's baby"— he opens his hands wide, and you realize he has been holding a photo cupped in them—"I'm just . . . I'm moved."

You look at the picture. But if you've seen one baby, you've seen them all. Squashy head. Floppy body. Hair optional. "Cute," you say, uninterested.

Xander comes back out of Ms. Belakane's office. "Hey," Oz greets him. "Want to see a picture of my cousin's baby?"

Xander walks over and glances at the photo. "Cute," he says.

"I'm gonna go see her. You guys could come," Oz offers.

"Okay," Xander says. "But could we get a pizza on the way? Or on the way back? Or both?"

"Now that you had your meeting with Ms.

Belakane, what do you think of her?" you ask. Because if he doesn't love her, you really don't know if you can be friends with him anymore.

"She is . . ." Xander throws his arms wide. "I can't come up with good enough words."

You nod, satisfied.

"So . . . baby?" Oz asks.

"Pizza?" Xander asks.

"What are we talking about . . . without me?" Willow asks as she joins the group. She looks at Oz, then looks away.

"Babies," Oz says.

"Pizza," Xander says.

"Oz wants to go visit his cousin's baby. Xander is down with visiting the baby, but wants pizza incorporated," you explain. "I'm thinking that Giles is waiting for me at this very moment."

"Oh, and I have research I want to finish on the—" Willow looks over at Oz. He doesn't know about the Slayage and all that goes with it. "You know, the green thing," she continues. "And then I'll want to discuss it with you, to up the Buffy safety factor."

Discussing. Uck. But training—which is why Giles is waiting for you—sounds perfect. The idea of getting in some punching and kicking is very appealing. You're a Peppie. It's your nature. Although pizza is good fuel. The protein and carbs allow for longer stretches of punching and kick—

A scream from outside jerks you out of your thoughts. You bolt to the closest window and stare over at the football field. Cordelia and Harmony Kendall are whaling away on the man who cuts the lawn and draws the chalk lines for games.

You bite your lip, uncertain. Should you go over there?

SLAYER CHOICE:

Do you decide to . . .

\ head over to the fight? *If yes, turn to page 100.*

\ go to the library to train with Giles? *If yes, turn to page 102.*

Oooh! Fight, fight, fight! You've got to get yourself over there! You bolt to the closest door and race out to the football field. Were you just talking to some people? Well, they can catch up if they want to. You're not a Mommie. You don't have to dress them up and put them in a stroller for a walk.

The school janitor is also running toward the fight. That's not right. He's an indoor guy. He's mop and bucket, cleaning up the puke and the overflowed toilet spillage. He shouldn't be on the field.

"Hey," you yell. "Back in your closet!" He doesn't listen. He should listen. Listening is an important skill. You tackle him. There are many other ways you could bring him to the ground, but you go with the football theme.

The janitor guy smells like bleach and dirty water, and hair gel, and something vomitous, and something even worse. You don't like it. "You should be inside," you tell him.

"Those girls are beating up Henderson," he says.

You keep your knee firmly pressed against his chest and look over your shoulder. "They aren't beating him up," you reply. "They are tying him to the goalpost with, I believe, a leather and ribbon belt, a suede belt, and some cheer lanyards." From the tiltage of the lawn-cutting guy's head, you suspect he has been sent to sleepy land for a little while. And you didn't get to help. Which is so unfair.

"Now are you going to go back inside?" you ask.

You sort of hope he says no, because you came out

here for the fight, fight, fight. But he says yes in a squeaky little voice. So you let him up and head over to Cordelia and Harmony. "Need any help?" you ask.

Harmony tightens the knot in the shoelaces she's used to lash the lawn dude's feet to the goalpost. "I think we got it," she says. "But I'll stand guard just in case."

"That guy wasn't enough of a challenge. I need to Bronze myself," Cordelia announces, dabbing the light sheen of sweat off her face with a tissue. "You want to come?" she asks, turning her beauty queen smile on you.

You glance back at the school building. Somewhere in there, Giles is waiting to train before his date.

But dancing is a workout too. Maybe you *should* go with Cordelia.

SLAYER CHOICE:

Do you decide to . . .

\ head over to the Bronze with Cordelia? *If yes, turn to page 105.*

\ go train with Giles? *If yes, turn to page 102.*

"**G**iles, I'm not going to bother buying you nice things if this is the way you're going to treat them," you say, because that's what your mother always says when your bedroom is a mess. And the training room? Big mess. Piles of books. Rolled-up mats. Groups of chairs. There is hardly enough space to walk.

"Because the Sleaninhnam will be appearing and disappearing into and out of dimensions, perhaps very rapidly, I want to concentrate on your footwork," Giles tells you. "So we'll do your usual fighting routine, while moving through the obstacles."

Giles straps pads on his arms and chest, and you're good to get Peppie. You start off with a nice front snapkick, followed up by a roundhouse kick that sends a pile of books smashing to the floor. Yeah!

"Buffy, the point of the obstacles is that they *are* obstacles," Giles tells you. "Remember, footwork."

But footwork isn't fun. Footwork isn't Peppie. You jab with your left, then your right. Giles comes at you. You leap up, roll off his shoulder, and slam into a group of chairs. You hurl yourself back to your feet and do a switch-step, trying to throw Giles off guard.

Then you throw a right cross to his jaw. Giles jerks back at the last second, and you miss. You don't usually go for the face during training. But it's good to mix things up in a fight.

"A little restraint, if you please," Giles chides. "And

concentrate on the footwork. The Sleaninhnam will require quickness on your part as well as strength."

You give Giles a double-fast right-left to the belly. You wish he wasn't wearing a pad. You know he needs the protection. But it's hard to tell that you've really landed a punch unless you *feel* the connection.

Front punch kick. Another. You back Giles into a pile of books. You use a shoulder block as he throws a right at your gut. You battle your way around the crowded room. Adrenaline pumps through your body with every thump of your heart. Big rush.

Giles's breath is getting ragged. You're still walking on those clouds. You don't feel like you need to breathe at all. You go for a hook to the jaw, holding back, even though you want to use every bit of muscle you've got.

Giles goes down. "I think that's enough for today," he says, wiping the sweat from his face with the back of his hand.

But it's not enough for you. You feel so incredibly, intensely alive!

You stride out of the training room.

Willow holds up a book. "I found something amazing!" she exclaims. "You have to hear this."

But you couldn't sit down in a chair and do the listening if you were paid a million dollars. The pep is roaring inside you.

What can you do next?

SLAYER CHOICE:

Do you decide to . . .

\ go try to find Ms. Belakane and tell her how satisfying it is to embrace your peppiness? *If yes, turn to page 244.*

\ go to the Bronze to dance off some of that excess energy that is still coursing through you? *If yes, turn to page 105.*

You step into the Bronze and let the thrashing music whip across you. This is definitely the right place to be. The Bronze vibrates with energy. Just the way you do. You head on out to the dance floor, groovin' in synch with Cordelia.

Cordelia is such a fabulous *chiquita*. You wonder why you don't spend more time with her. "Those boots are almost like the ones Ms. Belakane has," Cordy shouts over the music.

"Yeah," you answer. You don't even mind that your piggies are hating the dancing. You are loving your pointy-toed Ms. Belakane–like boots.

"Where'd you get them?" Cordy asks. Then she hurls herself into another dancer, even though you're not all that close to the mosh pit.

Your shoe secrets are Cordelia's shoe secrets. She's a fellow Peppie. You can just tell. "Shoe Circus," you yell back. "Kind of hidden. Back under those purses with the silk screening and the ugly."

Cordelia slams into someone else. It looks kind of fun. So you choose someone to crash into, adding just a minor snap-kick, which is actually a cool dance move.

You feel someone's eyes on you. Not the eyes of your recent crash test dummy. You scan the Bronze. "Ms. Belakane's here!" you tell Cordy.

Ms. Belakane gestures you over to her table. You don't have to be gestured twice. You rush over there, Cordelia right behind you. The seats on either side of Ms. Belakane are taken. One by Xander. And one by Oz.

"You smell nice," you say to Xander. You've never really noticed his smell before, but he must have started wearing aftershave or some other boy perfume. He nods. He can't speak. His mouth is too full of pretzels. He shakes the empty bowl at the waitress.

You realize Xander doesn't smell nearly as good as Ms. Belakane. You wonder if she got her perfume specially made—a signature thing. She puts her hand on yours. "Are you having fun, Buffy?"

That bubble bath inside feeling starts up again. You can almost feel the warm, soft, pretty bubbles popping inside you. Like a little bubble party. "Fun, uh-huh," you answer. You feel a hand on your shoulder and you stiffen. You jerk your head around— and see Angel standing behind you, all tall and strong, with his spiky hair and his brown eyes that always make you think of secrets that you have to know.

He leans down and whispers in your ear, "Isn't it about time to go patrolling?" The way he says "patrolling" makes it clear he's talking about making-out patrolling, not patrolling patrolling.

But you're not ready to leave. Ms. Belakane is about to tell everyone how she became interested in developing a self-esteem program for teens. You need to hear that. And you want Angel to get the chance to know Ms. Belakane. He's going to love her. Although you wish he'd taken a shower before he came out tonight. He's kind of stinky, and you don't want Ms. Belakane to think you hang out with a guy who allows himself to go out in public with the reeking.

"This is my friend Angel," you tell her, leaving out the "boy" in front of "friend," just in case she doesn't like him. You point Angel into an empty chair.

"A pleasure to meet you," Ms. Belakane says. Oz takes a piece of hamburger meat and pops it into Ms. Belakane's mouth. She smiles at him as she swallows, then tells him, "Thank you, Mommie."

Angel raises an eyebrow as part of his overall Mr. Disapproving face. You kick him under the table, maybe a little too hard. But he's a vampire with superhuman strength. He can take it.

"Oz, the other Dingoes are howling for you," Cordelia says. Oz feeds Ms. Belakane one more piece of hamburger, then slowly stands up and heads over to join his band up onstage. Cordelia moves into the seat next to Ms. Belakane with a hair flip–grin combo. You should be the one in that chair. You need to be close to her, in case something happens.

"Who wants to dance?" Ms. Belakane asks, as Dingoes Ate My Baby starts to play.

"I do!" Cordelia cries.

"I do!" you exclaim. You jump up so fast, you knock your chair over.

"I'm going to order another burger," Xander says.

Angel just looks at you. "You can dance with us if

you want," you say. He stands up without a word and walks toward the exit. He can be so broody sometimes. You follow Ms. Belakane out onto the dance floor. Instantly, almost every kid from Sunnydale High circles around her, like she's Julia Roberts or somebody. They all smell okay to you, so you let them get a little of the Ms. Belakane vibe.

Then the hair on your arms and the back of your neck stands up. Something's not right. Willow pushes through the crowd. You move between her and Ms. Belakane. "What?" you cry.

"The Sleaninhnam de—um, I mean, you-know-who—is on a rampage at the senior citizens' home," Willow shouts over the music. "You've gotta get over there right now!"

That sounds bad. You look over at Ms. Belakane. "Don't go, Buffy. This is a great song!" she says.

It *is* a great song. You love this song. And you love hanging with Ms. Belakane. This is the only place you want to be.

You keep dancing.

Willow grabs your arm. "Buffy, what are you waiting for?"

"I love this song," you tell her.

"People are dying! You've got to come with me," Willow begs.

She's probably right. But Ms. Belakane said not to leave. What should you do?

SLAYER CHOICE:

Do you decide to . . .

\ leave the Bronze to go fight the demon? *If yes, turn to page 226.*

\ stay with Ms. Belakane and dance? *If yes, turn to page 110.*

"Sorry, Will," you say. You throw your arms over your head and do the bump-bump-bump with Ms. Belakane. "This is a fab song. Maybe when a slow one comes on."

"They'll all be dead by then, Buffy," Willow says. Her green eyes shimmer with unshed tears, and you feel your heart slide in your chest. The way it always does when there's a slammin' bass line.

Willow turns and walks away.

The next song is just as groovalicious as the last one. You and Ms. Belakane's entourage dance the Dingoes' whole set. When they take a break, Oz comes over. "Are you sure we're not tiring you out?" he asks Ms. Belakane.

She smiles and gives his face a you're-such-a-lambie pat. You wish you had thought to ask if she was getting tired. "It probably is time for me to be getting home," Ms. Belakane answers. "Oz knows a little secret about me," she confesses. "I'm getting ready to have my babies."

You, Cordelia, and the rest of the group squeal. Even the guys let loose with the squealies. You can't think of anything that would give you better warm-and-fuzzies than the idea of Belakane babies. How cute are they going to be? So cute, that's how.

Ms. Belakane reaches out and touches Cordy and a few of the other cheerleaders. Then she touches you. Bubblicious Buffy. "Will you girls come by and make sure there are no party crashers tonight?"

Like she has to ask. "I'm your go-to girl," you

say. "Except, in this case, I'm coming to you."

Cordelia links arms with you, and Kathy Boutry grabs your free hand. You girl power on out to Ms. Belakane's sleek black SUV. Holly Charleston grabs shotgun, but you snag the seat right behind Ms. Belakane, which is almost as good. You lean your head against the leather driver's seat as she drives, and imagine that she's using you as support.

Too soon, she pulls into the school parking lot. She's a good driver, nice and smooth. When you start driving, you want to drive just like she does.

Ms. Belakane gets out of the car, and you try to climb over Cordy to get out of the SUV first, but she's faster. You and your friends follow Ms. Belakane—you wonder if she'd mind if you call her Victoria, or even Vicky, except no, she doesn't really seem like a Vicky—out to the football field.

"You boys can take a break," she calls to a group of football players and the captain of the debate team who are hanging out on the fifty yard line. As they stride off, you notice a perfectly round hole about as wide as a double manhole in the field. Pretty.

Ms. Belakane nods as she looks at it. "The workers have done a marvelous job," she says. Then she gives you and the other girls a wave and climbs inside.

What a cool little pad she has. It's exactly the kind of place you'd like to have when you finally manage to move out of the Mom Motel. So minimalist and uncluttered.

"I hate those crackers they have at the Bronze,"

Holly complains. "The sesame seeds always gets stuck in my teeth." She holds out her hand. "Floss?"

"I've got cinnamon," you offer. "Good tasting and good for the gums." You dig it out of your purse and hand it over.

Holly opens her mouth, and her bottom jaw just keeps on openin'. It drops about six inches straight down, showing off two long, curved black teeth.

"I like," Elise Pearson says.

"My dentist didn't tell me that was a possibility. Bleaching trays are his idea of high tech," Cordelia says, circling around in front of Holly to get a better look. "Do you have a card for your guy?"

"Yeah, an upgrade would be cool. But did it hurt? I'm not so much with the pain. At least not when a drill is involved," you say. You reach into your mouth and finger your teeth. And ouchies—they're sharp. You open your mouth, and it *opens* opens. Oh, nice. This will be excellent for keeping the party crashers out of the party. And the big jaw will be useful for when you really need to eat the sweet and the salty and the crunchy all at the same time.

"Wait. Everyone knows about these but me?" Cordelia asks.

You're about to tell her to do a self-dental exam. But you spy Angel heading in the direction of the field. That is badness on many levels. One, he's a crasher. And two, he only wants to come over here to fight with you.

Fighting sounds appealing. Your muscles are in the

mood for a little kicky, punchy. But that's not the kind of fighting Angel wants. He wants the "Why did you do that?" "You owe me an apology" "Why?" "Why?" Why?" and other boring words type of fight.

And no part of you is in the mood for that. You have a job to do here. You could duck under the bleachers and hide out until he takes his hurt and broody away. Or you could just go over there and face the boring words now. You'll have to do it sometime, anyway. It's not like you can avoid him forever—he's immortal.

SLAYER CHOICE:

Do you decide to . . .

\ avoid Angel and keep guard? *If yes, turn to page 114.*

\ meet up with Angel? Might as well have it out now. *If yes, turn to page 133.*

Yᵒu smile as you walk into school the next day.

Keeping watch over Ms. Belakane's sweet li'l bachelorette pad last night was such the fun fest—once you got rid of Angel. You're so grateful to Cordy and Harmony for helping to hide you from him.

And the best part? Later, you get to guard again. Except tonight you'll get to guard Ms. Belakane's private lounge. You can't wait to see it. And even better, she'll be in the lounge. Face time for the happy Buffy. You'll use the next couple periods for catnaps, and you'll be all set to be Ms. Belakane's number-one guard.

"A word please, Buffy."

You turn, and there's Giles. You can tell by his face that he doesn't want a word. He wants a lot of words. And none of them are going to be words you want to hear. Well, the "and"s and "but"s and "or"s are okay, but the ones between those ones? Not gonna be the good words.

"I'm kinda tired," you tell him. "Late night. And class starting. A mind is a terrible thing to waste and all."

"Library," he says. Then he turns and walks away, so sure that he'll follow you. And you do. 'Cause . . . he's Giles. And Ms. Belakane doesn't need you right now. And class is . . . class. Even words from Giles are better than class.

The second the big wooden library doors swing shut behind you, the words start. "Buffy, I need a precise explanation of what happened last night. Willow came to you at the Bronze and told you that the

Sleaninhnam demon was in the midst of killing the residents of the senior citizen center. And you—"

"I decided to stay at the Bronze and hang with Ms. Belakane," you interrupt him, to try to reduce the number of words this whole encounter is going to take. "I need a night off once in a while. And a really superior song was playing."

"A superior song," Giles repeats.

"Uh-huh," you say. "Do you think I could catch a few zeebies in here and you could write me a pass?"

"Buffy. People died last night. People will continue to die unless you take action. The Sleaninhnam demon will continue its killing spree until you stop it. Not to mention the nightly rise of Sunnydale's undead and their victims. This is a situation of the utmost seriousness. I must make a report to the Council. You need to help me understand," Giles continues, his eyebrows all furrowey. Which gives lines, permanent ones. But maybe when you're old and British, you don't care about things like that.

Finally he stops talking. It's your turn.

"Giles, demons kill people," you say. "So do vampires. It's what they do. I can't always be there. 'Cause I'm only one Buffy." And the one Buffy you are needs to be near Ms. Belakane.

Giles gapes at you. "Have you been experiencing any unusual symptoms? Fever? Chills? The desire to eat raw meat or ginkgo leaves?" he asks.

You were willing to give him a few minutes because he's Giles and because Ms. Belakane doesn't need you. But *you* need to rest up. You need to be in tip-top shape for your lounge-guarding later. You have no more time for this conversation. You turn toward the door, and—huge sigh—here comes Willow, dragging Xander behind her.

Willow gives you the eyes of accusation. She clearly doesn't understand priorities and that a Slayer has to have them. If you'd gone after the Sl-thing, you would have missed patrolling the pad. And if you hadn't been there, what if something bad-like had happened to Ms. Belakane?

"Good god," Giles exclaims. "What's happened to Xander?"

"I don't know," Willow answers. "Yesterday he had the extreme hungries. This morning . . ." She nods at Xander's middle. It's twice as big as the rest of his body. He doesn't have man breasts. But he has a man bosom—man breasts so big, they have fused together into a shelf, which has fused with his belly.

"Xander, excuse me, but would you, er, mind raising up that sweatshirt a bit?" Giles asks.

"Okay." Xander yanks it up to mid-humongous belly lump. The lump is the color of amber—pretty—and also sort of see-throughish. There is gooeyness underneath. It makes you feel . . . hungry.

"You do realize that what you are exhibiting is rather, um, unusual," Giles says.

"Xander, it's Guinness Book-worthy," Willow exclaims. "Remember the fingernails? It's worse than the fingernails! Tell him, Buffy."

"I'm likin' the new look." You pat the tum-tum. It's kinda reassuring.

Giles and Willow stare at you. Then they give each other one of those conversation looks—like the entire look is a conversation you aren't allowed to be in on. You know they're doing it, but you don't really care much.

"Do you think maybe I could go take a little nap now?" you ask.

"No. I need you here," Giles snaps. "Please." He turns to Xander. "Can you tell me when this desire to consume more food than usual began?"

"Sure. After I saw Ms. Belakane. She told me I'm a Teddie and—"

"Ms. Belakane. That woman's name comes up again and again," Giles interrupts. "I am going to go have a word with her this moment." He starts toward the door.

"No!" you cry, blocking him. "Ms. Belakane is busy. And besides, your smell would make her vomitous."

"My smell?" he repeats.

"Yeah. You smell all musty, like the books," you tell him.

He blinks at you. "Buffy, why don't you take that nap now? The chair in my office is especially comfortable. Willow and Xander will stay with you," Giles says. He tries to step around you.

You know where he's going. He's going to see Ms. Belakane. And you can't let him do that.

You use your body as a barricade.

"Come on, Buff," Willow pleads. "It'll be fun. A little sleepover at school. I can paint your nails. And we can watch one of the less-educational videos. It will be fun of the fun kind. Right, Xander?"

"Yep," Xander says. "Can we have popcorn?"

Willow keeps talking, but you focus all your attention on Giles. "You aren't getting anywhere near Ms. Belakane," you inform him.

"Buffy, step out of my way."

You don't. Giles shakes his head and tries to move around you. You turn and jab him in the stomach with your elbow. While he is bent over, you bring your other elbow down on the back of his head.

You slam your knee into his chin. "Buffy, stop!" Willow screams.

But you're not going to stop. Not until you know Giles won't be bothering Ms. Belakane. Now that his head is up, you give him your best hook to the jaw. He goes down. He'll be out for a while.

Maybe when he wakes up, he'll be less cranky. And he'll realize that you need to be able to spend time with other people—like Ms. Belakane—without him making some federal case out of it.

Clearly the library isn't going to be good for the napping. And class has already started. You're sure Ms. Belakane wouldn't mind if you crash out at her place. It's big enough to hold everyone she knows.

You turn toward Willow and Xander to tell them you're out. Willow has her back pressed up against

Giles's desk. She's staring at you like you're . . . something out of the really educational educational videos. Waves of hideous stink are coming off her. There's something wrong with her. She looks . . . crazed.

Willow shoves herself away from the desk and races toward the library doors.

Is she going after Ms. Belakane? 'Cause if she is, you have to stop her.

But Willow smells afraid. Maybe she's just running away. If so, you can let her go. You *do* need a nap, after all.

SLAYER CHOICE:
Do you decide to . . .

❙ stop Willow? *If yes, turn to page 120.*

❙ let her go? *If yes, turn to page 124.*

You can't let somebody that insane leave this room. It isn't safe for Ms. Belakane. "Willow, stop!" you order.

She doesn't.

You race after her, catching her by her hair. You spin her around to face you. Her eyes are wild. She is truly dangerous. Who knows what she might do to Ms. Belakane?

You take her throat in your hands. You squeeze. Willow flops and jerks like a puppet. Then she goes still.

But you just keep squeezing.

THE END

You've got to follow Ms. Belakane. You've got to see what's got everyone all gaga-gag over her. Especially a certain someone who should know better because he already has someone much better, thank you very much. Or will have, unless he keeps on paying a little too much attention to Miss Freakishly Big Eyes/Freakishly Low Body Fat.

And besides, your eyelashes are feeling puny. They are sobbing for some mascara, and so you need to go to the bathroom no matter who is in there. It's a public place. The use of it whenever your eyelashes are light is one of your basic human rights. It's probably in the Constitution, and if it's not, it should be. You think about asking Willow to come with you. But Oz's band is playing, and she probably wants to hear them.

You shoot her a quick glance. She's staring at the floor. But still, probably grooving on the inside. Right?

You head across the dance floor. The Dingoes sound as if someone really did eat their baby. Oz is clearly distracted and not playing very well. Sometimes he forgets to play at all. You step into the bathroom. Nobody in sight. Ms. Belakane must be in one of the stalls. You decide some snoopage of the stealth kind might be in order. So, quiet like a bunny, you get yourself into the closest stall and get your pretty and painful boots out of view by sitting on the toilet seat and pressing your feeties against the door.

A moment later, you hear the *click, click, click* of heels moving toward the sink. You realize you didn't hear the *whoosh* of water. She didn't flush. How

disgusting. You wonder what that certain male someone would think of that? You stand and step up to the
little open place at the edge of the door. You put your
eye up to it.

Ms. Belakane doesn't wash her hands, either.
That's something any certain male someone should
know before he even thinks about letting her put her
hands on him. Not that he's thinking about that. At
least you hope not. The thought does bad things to
your tummy. You try to erase it from your memory.

You watch as the one who should not even be at
the Bronze because of her oldness and teacherishness
pulls a Chanel lipstick out of her purse. She takes off
the cap, and you see that she's about to reapply that
come-to-hoochie-mama shade. ID of *under* 21 should
be required to buy a shade like that.

She drops it. Then she gives a little hum, like it's
no big deal. She doesn't even bother to pick it up. The
boosting of teen self-esteem must pay pretty well.
Because lipstick like that doesn't grow on trees. Or
even in Rite-Aid. You have to go to one of your better
shopping malls for that lipstick.

Ms. Belakane powders her face with one of those
cute little sheets that come in a tiny pack like little
Kleenex. You should ask her where she gets those. No.
Wait. You are waiting for her to peel back her face and
show her monster self. Or other badness. At least you
already have the no flushing and no hand-washing.
And the wastefulness. Leaving the lipstick on the
ground is—

The lipstick isn't on the ground anymore. It is sliding up the wall.

You press your eye against the crack and stare at the lipstick to be sure you aren't imagining things.

Nope. It's moving. Slowly, but moving.

What's going on? Witchcraft? Mind control? Except you can't use mind control on a lipstick, can you? Because a lipstick has no mind, right?

It has no mind, but it seems to have teeny weeny little legs as it marches across the sink and over to Ms. Belakane. She picks up the lipstick with her free hand, and you see a line of ants underneath. Teeny-tiny brown ants, at least fifty of them. They were the lipstick movers.

You watch as they march—not two by two, like in the song, but in orderly lines—down Ms. Belakane's body and into her purse.

And now you are well and truly freaked out. Because that? Was bizarre with a capital Biz.

You yank open the stall door and rush out of the bathroom. You'll just see if she's quite so attractive, and sweet, and smart, and whatever else Mr. Lovey Dovey Pants thinks she is once you tell him about this little episode.

SLAYER ACTION:
If Angel is here and acting weird,
turn to page 155.

If Giles is the one who's acting weird,
turn to page 220.

You watch Willow disappear through the library doors. Your nostrils flare as you determine that her stench is moving away from Ms. Belakane and not toward her. You'll have to keep a nose out for Willow and her craziness.

"Hey, Xan, want to go over to Ms. Belakane's?" you ask.

"Okay," Xander says. "I'm supposed to be over there in about an hour, anyway."

You head out to the football field. Four wrestlers stand along the fifty yard line, keeping watch. Emily Eiselin from the Young Businesswomen Club and Andy Hoelich from the gymnastics team guard the entrance. Andy does a happy flip when he sees you, and you and Xander climb into the hole and down the earth steps to the first tunnel.

The two of you hi-ho, hi-ho along, checking out the expansions Ms. Belakane's got underway. Your stomach starts to grumble and complain. "You want something to eat?" Xander asks.

"I did skip breakfast," you admit.

"Not a problem." Xander's belly rolls and heaves, then he does the Technicolor yawn into his hands. From the orangeness and the smell, it's clear Xander's been eating Cheez Doodles—one of your faves. You hold out your hands, and Xander passes the yum into them.

As the warm goop travels down your throat, you wonder why you've never thought about having someone chew your food for you before. It's so convenient. And it really brings out the flavor. "Thanks, Xan," you say.

"That's what I'm here for," he says. "Teddies are all about bringing food to the Mommies, and the Peppies, and the Smarties. You keep this place running."

"Aw, but we couldn't do it without you," you tell him. The tunnel opens to a cozy earth room. Nice and dim, with only little bits of light coming in from pinholes leading to the surface. "I'm going to take a dirt nap so I'll be ready to guard later," you tell Xander.

"Okey-dokey," he says. That's the kind of friend you need. The kind of friend who gets you. Who understands that what you do for Ms. Belakane is important.

You curl up in the corner. And when it's time to guard, you wake up. Just like that. No alarm necessary. You go down to level three, the lowest floor in Ms. Belakane's place. Wow. Her personal lounge is dazzling. Halogen lights everywhere. And it's like Pottery Barn exploded down here. It's extreme cool.

"Hello, Buffy," Ms. Belakane calls. She's lounging on a love seat with Principal Snyder. His mostly bald head is shining with sweat under all the lights. It's cute. You wonder if you should find a towel and pat it dry. But maybe Ms. Belakane would rather do that herself. She has made quite the invasion on his personal space. Her hands are cupping his temples.

An extra bright light catches the corner of your eye, and there's a crackling, whooshing sound. Did a bulb pop? You whip your head in that direction, wanting to make sure there's no danger.

And you see a humongous leprechaun coming toward you on a giant playground slide. Willow and Giles are right behind him.

It's not a leprechaun, you remember. It's a Sleaninhnam demon.

Thwomp! The demon lands hard enough to make Ms. Belakane's lovely cabinet/bookcase unit fall to the ground, breaking several of her little knickknacks. Your blood starts to boil. Well, not really, because then you'd be dead. But you are mad, and you are going to make him pay for that.

"So this is the little Slayer who's been too afraid to face me," the demon growls. His bright blue eyes twinkle with malice, and he gives the handle of the massive black mallet he's holding a loving pat. You suspect he has a pet name for the thing.

"Yep, there she is," Willow tells him. She turns to you, her green eyes anxious. "Buffy, isn't the evil demon too close to Ms. Belakane?"

"She won't even come after me now." The rosy-cheeked, all-green-wearing demon turns to Willow and Giles. "The two of you have wasted my time. I hate time wasters more than anything. Except yammerers and clumsy louts."

"Don't worry. I'm comin' after you. You just didn't do anything to piss me off before." You look at the crack in the red lacquered vase lying on the floor. The demon *is* way too close to Ms. Belakane. "Now you very much have."

A delicious smell fills the lounge. It makes you

want to kick the demon's big velvet-covered butt even more than you did two seconds ago. And that's saying a lot.

The demon thing swings his big black mallet over his shoulder like it's a baseball bat. Your first job: Get that thing out of commission. You let your jaw drop, and lunge at the demon's elbow—which is as high as you can reach—with your high-tech new teeth.

And whoops, there it is: the demon's mallet on the ground. Along with the hand that's holding it. And half the arm that's attached to the hand.

"I needed that!" the demon screams, looking at his mallet. "And that," he adds, moving his eyes up to his arm.

He lurches toward you. But Harmony, Cordelia, and Kathy fly into the lounge, wanting some of the fun. Even though you haven't had that much yet. You've gotten a yee, but definitely not a whole yee-haw.

Harmony bites off a leg. Cordelia bites into the belly and yanks some goo free. Kathy gets a hunk of the non-leprechaun's neck. You could bite off the demon's other arm, but he's already dead, so it wouldn't give so many giggles.

"Buffy! Buffy, help!" Willow shrieks.

Willow should be nowhere near Ms. Belakane. You spin around.

Ms. Belakane holds Willow in the claws of two of her six hairy black legs. Willow screams as Ms. Belakane's eyes grow farther apart. Her nose moves forward, turning a dark brown color. Antennae shoot straight up from her head. Her abdomen extends into a huge, swollen poison sac that feeds poison to a stinger at one end.

You stare at her. The sleek woman in the suit is gone. Ms. Belakane is a humongous black ant. Cool!

Belakane brings Willow toward her pincers. The black maw of her mouth is just behind them.

"Buffy, help me!" Willow screams. She locks eyes with you. "I don't want to die. Buffy, please!"

You feel something move in your chest. You kind of recognize the feeling. It's guilt . . . or worry . . . something like that. Willow's your best friend, and she's about to get eaten.

Or maybe you're just about to transform like Belakane?

"Buffffy!" Willow cries.

SLAYER CHOICE:

Do you decide to . . .

❙ stay where you are? Belakane can eat whomever she wants. *If yes, turn to page 129.*

❙ save Willow? *If yes, turn to page 130.*

"**B**uffy, help!" Willow screams.

You don't move. Cordelia comes to stand next to you. "Belakane needs protein," Cordy comments.

"Yeah, for all the little babies that are coming," Kathy agrees.

You nod. Protein is important.

Giles rushes toward Belakane. She grabs him in two of her free legs. Or are they arms? Whatever. She grabs him and still has two thingies to balance on.

Belakane puts Willow's head into her mouth. You hear a *crunch*. Then a *squish*.

Then silence.

THE END

Willow's voice reverberates through your brain. And it triggers memories. Willow being sweet, and friendly, and nerdy on your first day of school. Willow tracking you down to that frat party where you'd been chained to the wall as reptile food. Willow helping you with math, and English, and history. Willow covering up her hot Halloween costume with a head-to-foot ghost sheet. Vampires wanting to slit Willow's throat to use her blood to resurrect the Master. Willow listening to you babble about Angel for many, many hours.

Willow. Your best friend.

Willow.

Belakane is going to kill Willow!

"No!" you shout.

You run at Belakane, leap into the air, and slam both of your feet into her abdomen. She spits Willow out.

Cordelia, Harmony, and Kathy scream in fury. Belakane snatches you with her two closest legs. "Block the entrance," you call to Willow and Giles. "Backup guards will be coming."

Then you twist your body so you're facing down. You let your jaw drop, and you use your fang-pincers—gross, but useful—to slice into the huge poison bag that makes up the bottom third of Belakane's body. Cordy and her two Cordettes throw themselves back against the wall to avoid the acid spew.

Belakane jerks you up toward her mouth. Just what you were hoping she'd do. You grab one of her pincers with both hands and snap it free. Belakane howls in pain and fury. You see yourself reflected in each section of her multifaceted eyes.

You pull your arm back. And you stab one of the Buffys in her eyes as hard as you can.

Then you're on the ground. And Belakane is nothing but a big grease spot underneath you.

"Are the walls of this place made of *dirt*?" Cordelia asks, sounding completely disgusted.

You try to drop down your jaw. It goes about three inches. And your teeth—as far as you can feel—are mostly blunt. You scan the lounge, you have to find—

"Willow?" you cry. You take a step toward her. Is she even your friend anymore? She rushes over to you and gives you a hard hug. Your legs go all wobbly, and you have to sit down.

Giles walks over and kneels down in front of you. "Are we underground?" you ask. Your brain is feeling all confuzled.

"Yes," your Watcher tells you. "And I think the first thing we should do is get everyone back into the sunlight."

You look around. "Did they open a Pottery Barn down here?" Giles helps you to your feet. "Come along, girls," he says to Cordelia, Kathy, and Harmony. He leads you out of the bright room into a dim tunnel. Willow stays close beside you.

You keep seeing kids from school. Which is weird. Was there some kind of field trip? You can't remember. There isn't much to see. Dirt and more dirt. Giles herds everybody along, making you all walk uphill.

"Hey, there's Xander!" Willow exclaims. "Xander, over here."

Xander joins the little cluster of you, Willow, and Giles. "Can someone explain why I feel like I've been in a pie-eating contest, except the part about the pie?" he asks.

Giles and Willow look at each other. "No idea," Giles says.

"What time is it?" you ask. "Am I supposed to be training? I can't remember what I'm supposed to be doing. It's like I've been doing fifty things at the same time or something."

"I believe the last time we spoke, you mentioned something about a nap," Giles says. "I think that would be a suitable course of action at the moment. Perhaps for all of us."

"Anything that's not a picnic is good for me," Willow says.

You stare at her, baffled. So does Xander.

But Giles laughs . . . until he catches sight of your expression. "Picnic," he says. "Ants. Because they frequent picnics."

You and Xander keep staring. Is this some British thing? Why is he talking about ants?

"Oh, never mind," Giles says. He puts his arm around your shoulder. "I'm just glad to have you back."

THE END

Y ou may as well deal with Angel now. You don't want him following you around for the rest of your life. Forget about his. You stride across the football field and cut him off before he can step foot on it.

"You're mad because I didn't want to make out with you," you say, just to speed things along. You want to get back to the field. You're too far away from the entrance to Ms. Belakane's colony.

"I wanted to see you," he says. He looks at you with his big, sad, brown cow eyes. "And I thought you might want company when you patrol."

"I have company." You point toward Cordelia and the rest of your new crew.

"That's where you're patrolling? The football field?" he asks.

"And what's underneath it," you tell him.

"What's underneath it?" he asks.

"Angel, just because we hang out sometimes doesn't mean you get to know everything about my life. It's not like you've told me every detail of your existence," you answer. "And, also, I did ask you to stay and dance, even though you didn't bother to take a shower, so you didn't have to come over here all cow eyes."

"How do you know that woman you were with tonight?" Angel asks.

"Ms. Belakane? Don't you love her? She's doing a self-esteem workshop at the school," you tell him. "Did you notice that she has boots that are almost exactly like mine?"

Angel stares at you for a long moment. "I didn't

get to talk to her much at the Bronze. And since you like her so much, I'd like to get to know her. Do you think you could take me to her?" he asks.

Huh. You get the feeling that he's lying. But his smell is the same as it was before. Maybe you can't smell it when vampires lie? Whatever. You don't really know why he'd want to meet Ms. Belakane.

Then again, what harm could it do? You'd be there to protect her, just in case. And maybe she'd like to meet him.

SLAYER CHOICE:

Do you decide to . . .

\ stop him from going anywhere near Belakane? *If yes, turn to page 135.*

\ take him to Belakane? *If yes, turn to page 137.*

Your internal lie detector goes off.

Boing!

You don't believe Angel wants to meet Ms. Belakane because you like her so much. You don't know why he wants to meet her, but that isn't it. Maybe he wants to kill her. Or even just hurt her. Doesn't matter what he wants, really. There's no way you're letting him get anywhere near her.

"No," you tell him.

"Buffy, I'd really like to get to know her better," Angel insists.

Boing!

Something's wrong. Something's bad wrong. You reach into your coat. Good thing you always keep a stake. You slide it free and raise it, aiming at his heart.

Angel grabs you by the wrist, locking the stake in the air. You slam your free hand into his belly quick and hard, one-two. Then you use your new fangs— longer and at least as sharp as his—to tear into his flesh from his shoulder to his ribs.

He hisses with surprise and pain, and his grip on your wrist loosens. You spin away from him, then leap up, kick out, and slam your boot into his jaw. You follow that up with a roundhouse kick, connecting with his jaw again.

"Buffy, I don't want to hurt you," Angel says.

No boinging.

He means that. He really doesn't want to hurt you. You can use that. You drop the stake and go at him with a left hook–side-kick combo. He grabs your leg and jerks, bringing you to the ground.

Then he's coming down on top of you. He's going to use the weight of his body to pin you to the ground. Because he doesn't want to hurt you.

You're ready for him. You snatch the stake—you fell exactly where you wanted to. He won't be a threat to Belakane when he's dead.

You point the stake at Angel's heart as he brings his body down to meet it.

THE END

Angel and the persistence. He's going to be after you every night. *Can I see Ms. Belakane? Can I see Ms. Belakane?* You might as well just take him there now.

"Look, I'll try to get you in there," you say. "But if Ms. Belakane doesn't want company, then that's it."

"Fine," Angel says.

You march him across the football field. "Ms. Belakane has a visitor," you tell the others. "I'll escort him. Make sure he's not a crasher."

Cordelia doesn't look happy. But she might just be annoyed that you're going to get a little extra Belakane time. She steps away from the hole. You climb down the steps that have been carved into the earth.

The earth tunnel you find yourself in is so cozy—narrow, but tall enough for you to stand up in. Angel has to duck his head a tiny bit. It's really dark inside, but you don't need to see. The scent of Ms. Belakane's signature perfume leads your way. You wonder what it's called. Maybe Just Me! Or Queen of Everything.

The tunnel widens into a small room, and you see Matt Lopez from the Model UN Club and that dweeby guy Andrew Wells digging away to make it even bigger. They have nifty claws on the end of their arms. Ms. Belakane's clearly giving all her peeps upgrades. "Hey, guys!" you say as you pass by.

You keep heading toward the nose yum, which is coming from level three. Your stomach growls. You didn't eat anything at the Bronze.

"Hey, Buff. You hungry?" a familiar voice asks.

You peer into the darkness and see Xander. *He* has clearly showered today, unlike some people—or vampires. He smells very nice. "I am kinda hungry," you answer.

"Not a problem." Xander pats his belly. It's big and round like an XXXL Santa's. Except, unlike Santa's, you can sort of see through it. It's adorable. As you watch, the Xander belly rolls and heaves, then he does the Technicolor yawn into his hands. You hold out your hands, and Xander passes the yum into them.

Angel makes a coughing/gagging sound as you slurp up the food. He gets very interested in the dirt of the dirt wall.

"Thanks, Xan," you say.

"That's what I'm here for," he says. "Teddies are all about bringing food to the Mommies, and the Peppies, and the Smarties. You keep this place running."

"Aw, but we couldn't do it without you," you tell him. You walk faster as you leave Xander. You're getting very close to Belakane now.

Yes. Here it is. Her personal lounge. It's dazzling. The light from dozens of halogen lamps fill the large dirt room. And it's like Pottery Barn exploded in here. Cool. Ms. Belakane lounges on the sofa in a pair of silk pajamas and files her nails.

"Ms. Belakane, my friend Angel wanted to talk to you. I told him that it was only okay if you weren't busy and you felt like talking. To him," you say in a rush. Maybe this wasn't such a great idea. You probably shouldn't be interrupting Belakane's alone time.

"Come in," she says, her eyes sliding up and down Angel's body. She sits up and pats the sofa. "Sit right next to me, Angel."

"Go, Angel," you say, when he doesn't immediately go to her. He walks over and sits on the couch.

Ms. Belakane smiles at you. "Thanks, Buffy. You've saved me a lot of bother." She reaches over to Angel and takes his head in her hands, her fingers digging into his thick brown hair. "It's so hard for a girl to find a mate these days."

She brings her face close to his, her mouth a breath away from his. She stares into his eyes. How great, you think. Angel's going to be Ms. Belakane's boyfriend.

Suddenly, Ms. Belakane jerks her hands off Angel. "Vampire!" she says, her nose wrinkled in disgust.

He smiles at her. "Buffy was right. You're amazing. I love you."

You knew he'd feel that way if he just spent a few more minutes with her. You were right to bring him down here.

Except . . . Belakane seems pretty pissed off. "You have wasted my time," she snaps. "You have no life force to give my babies. You're a worthless husk!"

Her nose wrinkles again as it moves forward, turning a dark brown color. Her eyes grow farther apart as antennae shoot straight up from her head. A pair of long, segmented black arms rip through the top of her silk of her pajamas. The bottoms rip completely off as her abdomen extends into a huge, swollen poison sac that feeds poison to a stinger at one end.

You stare at her. The sleek woman is gone. Ms. Belakane is a humongous black ant. Cool!

Angel doesn't struggle as she grabs his head and thrusts it into her mouth. There's a *crunch* sound. Then a *squish*.

Then silence.

THE END

"**I** think there are bigger badnesses going on than the Sleaninhnam demon," you tell Willow. "There was no giant leprechaun hopping around out on the quad, but there was definitely something wonky happening."

"But the dreams . . . Are you sure?" Willow asks.

"Don't worry. I'll be extra-strength careful," you promise.

Willow nods. "I'll go see what else I can find out. I still have some pages to read. I think I was about to get to the good part." She turns around and heads toward the library.

You start toward the closest exit. Then you hesitate. Maybe the place you need to patrol is right here. Inside the school. After all, it was all those Teddies and Mommies and Peppies causing the problems today. And there weren't any Teddies and Mommies and Peppies before Ms. Belakane showed up.

There wasn't a flirty, leave-y boyfriend, either.

You decide to patrol yourself down to Ms. Belakane's temporary office. You hope she won't be around. No Ms. Belakane means no one to stop you from snooping around in her files. You'd like to get a look at whatever it says in her records on Xander and Cordy, not to mention all the other suddenly crazy people at school.

A whooshing sound, accompanied by a rush of air, makes the back of your shirt ripple. You spin around. And there he is—the Jolly Green Leprechaun. Except he doesn't look jolly. He looks like a cranky baby with his rosy cheeks and big frown. An eight-foot-tall cranky baby.

"You were thinner in my dreams," you tell him.

"Reality adds ten pounds," he snaps.

"Is there any chance we could reschedule?" you ask.

He makes a little peace sign-y gesture with his hand, and another bright light appears. A golden slide whooshes through the light. The demon leaps onto it . . . and he's gone. Huh. Very cooperative of him.

Whoosh! Brilliant light flashes in front of you. And here he comes again. Sliding down another golden beam. This time you get your eyes off his face and see the massive mallet he has in his hand.

You aren't armed for patrol, because, well, you're in the middle of the school. You have a stake. *A* stake. As in one. You always have one. But that's it.

Mr. Lucky Charms raises the mallet. You drop to the ground as he brings it down and roll left as it smashes into the floor right beside you, cracking the linoleum and smashing the cement underneath.

You pull out your stake and jam it into his hand where it holds the mallet handle. The Sleaninhnam roars in pain and backhands you with his staked hand. You fly across the hallway and slam into a row of lockers. This thing is *strong*.

The Sleaninhnam grunts as he tries to free his mallet from the floor. He's still got your stake in his flesh, but he doesn't seem to mind it. You're defenseless.

Didn't Willow say she had need-to-know info on this guy? You really need to know it right about now. You decide this is one of those situations where it's better to run and live to fight another day—after finding out from Willow how to kill this eight-foot monster.

You race down the hall. You hear the *whoosh*. Bright light right in front of you blinds you for a second, and when you can see again you realize that the Sleaninhnam demon is coming down his golden beam face-first. The mallet is already raised. It's so huge, it obscures everything else from your vision.

There's no time to react. It's coming down. It's all you can see.

And then everything goes black.

THE END

"Angel, no!" you cry.

Belakane grabs his face in both her hands. She breathes in as if she's inhaling the most heavenly scented coffee in the world. Her eyes are wide. It's a total rush for her.

And for Angel, apparently. He wears a big goofy grin as he lets her . . . smell him.

Then Belakane's eyes narrow in fury. She pushes Angel's head away from her and leaps off the couch. "You have nothing for me!" she shrieks. Drops of spittle fly out of her mouth. They hiss and boil when they hit the earth. "You have no life to give to my children, vampire!"

SLAYER ACTION:
Turn to page 145.

The whites of Belakane's eyes disappear as the irises split again and again. Angel is reflected in each black surface. He steps toward her. "I'll give you whatever you ask," he promises.

The pleading sound in his voice makes your stomach turn. But before you can do anything, another sound catches your attention. Footsteps. Lots of them. Coming toward you. You dash to an end table and get ready to hurl it toward the entrance to Belakane's love chamber. But the face you see in the doorway is Willow's. Giles is right behind her. You've never been happier to see your friends.

"Don't hurt me!" Willow cries, holding up her hands.

You put the end table back down.

"No, no! Throw it!" Giles commands you, racing into the room. "They're right behind us!"

"The cheerleaders," Willow squeaks.

So you toss the table into the entrance. You race back to the sofa. Giles joins you and grabs the other end. You add it to the barricade.

You whirl back to face Belakane. She's advancing on Angel. And he's smiling at her. "You've wasted my time," she tells him. "I have a colony to build, and you've wasted my time."

There is a cracking, crunching sound . . . and Belakane's jaws snap out. They are as sharp and jagged as a saw blade. She tosses her head, her long black hair spilling down her back. Then she curves one finger at Angel. "Come here," she orders.

"Angel! Get away from her," you cry.

But he doesn't seem to care that Belakane's body is changing. Her dark eyes widen . . . literally. The eyes grow farther apart as her nose moves forward, turning a dark brown color. Antennae shoot straight up from her head. Her arms lengthen, becoming segmented black legs. Her abdomen extends into a huge, swollen poison sac with a stinger on one end.

You stare at her. The sleek woman in the suit is gone. Belakane is a humongous black ant.

Belakane attacks Angel.

You leap between him and Belakane and feel a blade cut through your shirt and into your back as her jaw slashes you. Angel grabs your arm and throws you to the ground.

"What are you doing?" you cry.

"I can't let you hurt Belakane," he says in a monotone. He steps over you, and Belakane's hand—well, *claw*—seizes him by the arm.

You whip your head toward Giles and Willow. They're fighting to keep any of Belakane's cheerleader army from crossing the barricade.

Wildly you scan the room. Weapon. You need a weapon. You grab one of the halogen torchiere lamps that light the room. You swing it though the air and let it fly. It hits one of the antennae that have sprouted from Belakane's head, and she whistles in pain.

Angel turns and stalks toward you. His face vamps. Uh-oh.

"I told you not to hurt her," he snarls. "Now you're going to pay."

He reaches for your neck. You go limp, putting up no resistance, and you fall to the floor, your bodies twisting together.

You reach for the stake you know Angel always carries inside his leather jacket, and pull it free. You twist and hurl it at Belakane. There is nothing human left in her, but Angel still seems to think he loves her. He hurls himself after the stake, trying to catch it.

But he's too late. The stake sinks into her body, and she howls.

Then she goes silent.

And Angel looks at you. Really looks at you. His eyes are back to normal. Back to being filled with love for you. Whatever mojo Belakane has been using on him is gone.

"So are brunette ants more your type?" you ask.

He answers by kissing you. And kissing you. And kissing you.

"This is making me want to hurl," Xander says.

You break away from the kissing long enough to look up. Willow, Giles, and Xander are all watching you. Behind them, a bunch of baffled-looking kids from school are wandering around the dirt hallway. Their mouths are all normal, and Xander's enormous stomach has disappeared.

There's going to be a lot of "explaining" to do once you all get back up to the surface. But for now, you kiss Angel just one more time.

You've earned it.

THE END

"**S**orry, Will. I've got itchy feet. I think I'm gonna patrol," you tell Willow.

Willow's face falls. "But the itchy feet—they could be used for dancing," she says.

"I just feel like I should be out there," you explain. "Maybe I'll meet up with you later." Or maybe you'll happen to meet up with Angel later, as you often happen to do, because he just happens to somehow know where you are. There are benefits to having a vampire for a boyfriend. And you do think of him as a boyfriend, even though he is more than two hundred years old. You will never think of him as your manfriend. The sound of that is yuck.

"But we're still going to the Bronze, right?" Xander asks.

"Well . . ." Willow looks a little lost.

"Yes," you tell her. "You're going. And you're wearing your cute blue T-shirt."

"Ooh, the one with 'Underdog' on it?" She sounds happier already.

"That's the one," you tell her.

"But you'll be the one saving the day," she jokes. "You know? 'Cause Underdog . . ." She gives it up.

"Have fun," you say.

When you head out to patrol that evening, you decide to start with the small children's cemetery. You haven't made a pass through there in a while, and the thought of anything foul in there is particularly unacceptable. But there is some daylight left, so you decide to take the long way. The long way that passes by many cute shoes peeking out of windows on Main Street. Because these boots have really got to go.

You hit the first store window and stop to study the goodies. Willow can have her math books. *This* is your favorite kind of studying. Your eye is drawn to a soft pink shoe that is very like a ballerina slipper. Nice wide toes. Mmmm. Much room for the piggies. And you enjoy the idea of a demon getting kicked in the face with such an adorable shoe. But the softness is a drawback in your line of work. Some of those demon mugs have spikes and other ouchables poking out of them. They'd slice right through the slipper. You sigh and move on.

Next store. Different shoes. Maybe those ones that look like Mary Janes from hell. Nothing would get through those. And you'd be tall when you were wearing them. Tall-ish. But is the clunk factor too—

You are pulled out of your thoughts by the sound of glass breaking. You jerk your head toward the sound and see a blond girl in a halter top lying on the sidewalk across the street. That's odd. Cordelia leaps through the smashed window of Bits of Trash a second later. That's even odder. She jams her knee on the blond girl's chest, her dark hair sweeping down on the girl's face.

"I told you I saw those earrings first!" Cordelia grabs a piece of glass from the ground and holds it to the girl's neck. "Now give them to me."

You dash across the street.

"There was another pair right next to them," the

girl answers in a trembling voice as you jerk Cordy's
wrist behind her back to make her drop the glass shard.

Suddenly Harmony Kendall, one of Cordelia's fol-
lowers, leaps through the broken window. "Hey!" she
yells. "Let go of Cordy, Freakshow." She brings her
hand up and hits you in the jaw. You are shocked. You
would have bet Harmony would not even be able to
deliver a decent slap. And her punch? Not so strong.
But it's the *idea* of her punch that's so shocking.
Cheerleaders don't punch people. That's your job.

The blond girl gets up and takes off down the
street.

Cordelia twists free of you and runs back into the
store. "I'd like to buy these earrings," she calls cheerfully.

Harmony shoves you out of her way. "And do it
fast, minimum-wage drone," she calls through the
busted window at the cashier. "We have a manicure
appointment in two minutes." She starts after Cordelia.

Uh-uh. Nobody socks you and then goes shopping.
You jump through the window and grab her by the
elbow. She turns and swings at you again.

You're still so shocked that you don't even block
it. She hits you in the jaw. It stings. You flick your finger in her face, right between the eyes, just hard
enough to hurt. Okay, maybe a leeetle bit harder.

That's when Harmony opens her mouth—wide—
and hisses at you. Her teeth look weird. Black weird.
All the money in the world and she doesn't go to the
dentist?

"I'm sorry. Did you just hiss at me?" you ask.

She does it again. It was a definite hiss.

"Done paying," Cordelia sings, coming up behind Bizarro Harmony. "Let's hit the Bronze."

Harmony closes her mouth and turns to Cordelia. "What about the manicure?"

"I'm more in the mood to dance," Cordelia says. "Aren't you? I'm just so *pumped*!"

They take off without even glancing at you. As if their behavior was totally normal. Which, for them, is just barely possible.

"I put the window on the card too," the cashier calls after her.

"Whatever," Cordelia answers as she crunches her way over the broken glass.

And suddenly a trip to the Bronze seems like a good idea. You did tell Willow and Xander you might catch up to them there. You can spare a little hanging-out time. And besides, you have a feeling the Cordelia weirdness is about to get weirder.

You stare down at the broken glass as you start after Cordy. A row of ants are climbing over what must be to them jagged glass mountains. You frown. The ants are moving in a perfect line. You don't spend a lot of your time studying ants, because, hello, there are many more interesting things to study—like almost everything. But you're pretty sure the walking-on-the-edge-of-a-ruler straightness is weird.

And the fact that a group of ants are carrying a credit card? Definitely weird.

You watch as the ants march, march, march into the Squeeze Me juice shop next door. Ms. Belakane stands next to the cash register. The credit card inches its way up the bright orange counter and over to Ms. Belakane's hand.

The Cordelia weirdness may be about to get weirder. But the Ms. Belakane weirdness is off the charts. You head into Squeeze Me just in time to see the girl behind the counter grab a grubby dish towel and smack down about five inches of the row of ants.

Ms. Belakane lets out a shriek of fury. Two arms tear through her neat little suit. Thin black arms with hair like wire. She uses those arms to grab Counter Girl around the neck.

You think the use of the grubby dish towel was gross too. But that doesn't mean Ms. Belakane gets to go all chokey. You cartwheel across the floor and land a kick on the back of Ms. Belakane's neck. She releases the girl and spins to face you.

Her dark eyes widen . . . literally. The eyes grow farther apart as her nose moves forward, turning a dark brown color. Antennae shoot straight up from her head. Her abdomen extends into a huge, swollen poison sac with a stinger on one end.

You stare at her. The sleek woman in the suit is gone. Belakane is a humongous black ant.

While you're staring, Belakane spits with rage. Droplets of the spit hit your leather jacket and burn tiny holes right through. Note to self: Don't let any of that stuff get on your face. It's way too strong for an acid peel.

You backflip out of spit range, snatch up one of the orange plastic chairs, and hurl it at Belakane. She barely reacts as it bounces off her shoulder. Why couldn't this place have real furniture?

Fast as a bullwhip, one of Belakane's thick arms— or are they legs—flashes out, twines around one of your calves, and jerks you off your feet and onto your back.

You jerk up your free leg, pointing the heel of your boot at her throat. She hurls herself at you—and impales herself. Leaving a puddle of goo for Counter Girl to mop up.

You're liking these shoes a lot more than you were ten minutes ago. They still hurt your piggies, but they saved your bacon.

THE END

Y ou head straight for Angel to tell him about the lipstick. And the ants. And the lipstick *with* the ants.

But Angel isn't there. Willow's still there staring sadly into space. Xander's still there shoving food into his face. Cordelia's still slam dancing, even though the Dingoes are playing some kind of ballad.

But no Angel. It's an Angel-less Bronze.

Your heart gives a little squeeze. He's gone? Without you? He didn't even bother saying good-bye. He didn't even let you tell him about how his she's-so-sweet has very un-sweet hands and doesn't bother flushing, which is not at all thoughtful for the next person.

He didn't get to hear about her bug fetish. Or the bugs' fetish for her. You're not really sure which it is.

You sigh. Angel just has to be all mysterious and serious and disappear into the shadows all the time like he has something better to do.

Well, you can find something better to do too.

Like . . . go home.

SLAYER ACTION:
Turn to page 27.

You cross the street and take cover under one of the trees across the street from Angel's apartment. There's something going on with your broody boyfriend, and you're going to find out what. Even if you have to wait here all night.

Luckily, you don't. You only have to wait about an hour. An hour spent trying to figure out what is going on inside Angel's mind. Never an easy job. But tonight? Your basic impossible.

Angel's door opens. He's on the move. On the move in his cute midnight blue shirt—which does not seem good to you. Who is he wearing his cute shirt for, if not you? He strides off down the street with his long legs. You follow him, careful not to get too close.

The streets are familiar, and you have a bad feeling you know just where he's going. Finally he cuts across the Sunnydale High parking lot. You can think of only one reason for Angel to show up at the high school in his blue shirt that makes his chest look so wide. And that reason is named Ms. Belakane. She must be working late tonight—and obviously Angel knows it. Do they have a date or something?

Angel is already halfway across the parking lot, walking fast. You follow him. Normally he'd notice someone trailing him, but obviously his mind is on other things—or another *person*. He doesn't even glance over his shoulder. He heads directly to the football field.

Huh. Maybe you're wrong about him. If he was here for Ms. Belakane, why would he be going to the football field? You let him walk out onto the field while you hang back and take in the scene. Cordelia and her court of cheerleaders are spread out across the fifty yard line, like they're waiting to be judged for the Miss America pageant. Okay. That's weird. What are they doing here? And there's something . . . wrong . . . with their faces. Their mouths. Are they chomping on massive jawbreakers or wads of gum or what? Very unattractive. You'll have to take off points for that.

You stay by the bleachers till you can figure out what's what. All the girls snap into motion when Angel gets close to them. But they aren't building a pyramid or doing a cheer. They're down on their knees, pawing at the grass. And it's coming right up. You realize that a hole has been dug into the football field.

And your boyfriend is climbing down into it.

SLAYER ACTION:
Turn to page 163.

Your body temperature drops. You wrap your arms around yourself. It doesn't help. You can't watch this. You can't. In one more second, Belakane will be kissing Angel and it will kill you.

You turn and run back down the tunnel as fast as you can.

A horrible shriek stops you. "You are useless to me," you hear Belakane scream. "You have no life to give my eggs, vampire!"

Well, that doesn't sound good. You spin around and race back toward Angel. You hear a sickening crack. You round the corner.

And you see Belakane on top of Angel. She's broken off the wooden leg of the coffee table—and she's about to stab it into Angel's heart.

He smiles up at her, his eyes on her face.

He is powerless against her, you realize. He thinks he loves her.

And you love him more than you have ever loved anything. But you're too late to save him.

THE END

"**T**ell you what," you say. "If you guys want to research, great. I'll just go find Ms. Belakane and see what's what. Then if you come across any useful tidbits, you'll come find me."

"Buffy, it could be dangerous," Giles warns you. "We don't have any idea what we're dealing with here."

"I'll be careful," you promise. "Recon only."

But as you leave Giles's apartment, you check your jacket for a stake. If you find Ms. Belakane and she's doing anything remotely demonish, you're going to kill her. Period.

Now . . . where to start? The only places you've ever seen Ms. Belakane are at school and at the Bronze. School is closer. You doubt there's much chance that she'll still be in her borrowed office this late at night. But it's possible, since she's so, so, so concerned about the poor, traumatized kids of Sunnydale High. And since that's a big, fat lie. She could be using her office as the staging ground for . . . whatever evil plan she's got going.

Behind you, you hear a door close. You turn to see Xander heading out of the courtyard in front of Giles's place. Does he want to do recon with you?

No. He heads toward the little convenience store at the end of Giles's street.

You decide you can't worry about him right now. He'll probably just stay where he is until he's eaten through Sunnydale's supply of chips and cookies. Your job is to find Ms. Belakane and figure out how Xander got this way in the first place.

You head to Sunnydale High without much hope. But you get lucky. You see a light on in the office next to Principal Snyder's, and that's the office Ms. Belakane is using to dispense self-esteem. And possibly something not so nice. You flash on Xander and his giant see-through-ish belly. Ugh. This is not the time to be thinking of him. You need to focus on the task at hand.

You creep up to the office window, staying low, and peer in. Is Ms. Belakane going over test scores? Is she deep in thought about how to help some poor self-loathing teen? No, she's putting on some dark red lipstick. Possibly Cherries in Snow. Which—good choice. It looks amazing on her. And now she's letting her hair out of that bun. It falls down her back in long, black waves. Clearly, Ms. Belakane has plans. You just hope they don't include your boyfriend.

She stands up and pulls on a tight leather jacket, which is sort of like yours. Which is totally wrong. She should not get to be dressing from the Buffy department. She flicks off the light. You figure she'll leave by the door closest to the parking lot. That's the one the janitor keeps open late. Sadly, you've been at school late often enough to know these things.

You circle around to the parking lot. You're surprised to see a bunch of cars in the lot. Maybe a swim team bunch. Or a mathlete competition bunch. But the school is dark, so you know none of these things is actually happening. You add the cars to your mental list of the weird. And your mental list of the helpful.

Because the cars? Perfect cover. You hide behind one of them and wait for Ms. Belakane to come out. And you realize, way too late, that Ms. Belakane's going to be driving away from you in about five seconds. It sucks not being able to drive!

The back door to the school swings open, and you see Ms. Belakane stride out. Her hair is bouncin' and behavin'. She could be in a shampoo commercial. You wonder if you'd have time to crawl into the backseat after she hits the car door opener thingie, but before she reaches the car. You scan the lot, trying to match Ms. Belakane to one of the vehicles.

But, hey. She's not stopping at the lot. Is she walking home? What's she doing? Well, that's what you're here to find out. You let her get a head start, then you follow her . . . to the football field.

"Okay. That's . . . unexpected," you mutter. She doesn't seem like the rah-rah type. Especially the late-night, abandoned-field kind of rah-rah.

Except the field is not so much abandoned. Cordelia and her court are spread out across the fifty yard line, like they're waiting to be judged for the Miss America pageant. Okay. That's weird. What are they doing here? And there's something . . . wrong . . . with their faces. Their mouths. Are they chomping on massive jawbreakers or wads of gum or what? Very unattractive. You'll have to take off points for that.

You hang back by the bleachers till you can figure out what's going on. Is Ms. Belakane holding a late-night practice for the Peppies? She strides across the field, somehow managing to not get her stilettos caught in the ground. Cordelia and the other girls snap into motion when Ms. Belakane reaches them. But they aren't building a pyramid or doing a cheer. They're down on their knees, pawing at the grass. And it's coming right up. You realize that a hole has been dug into the football field. Snyder's not gonna like that.

Ms. Belakane walks past Cordelia and Harmony, who practically kiss her feet as if she's in charge of the whole pageant. She climbs down the hole in the football field and disappears.

SLAYER ACTION:
Turn to page 163.

You've got to get yourself down that hole. But Cordy and the Cordettes are obviously guarding it.

You need a plan. How hard can it be to outsmart Cordelia? Especially Cordelia the way she's been acting lately—high on the pep, low on the brains. Surprise is going to be key. You duck under the bleachers. Oh, yuck. And gather up some bottles and cans. Even more yuck.

Rapid-fire, you hurl bottles and cans in all directions. The line of guards along the fifty scatter to investigate. Cordelia and Kathy Boutry remain near the hole. Two other cheerleaders take positions about twenty feet to either side of it. You know the ones who took off will be back quickly. You run as fast as you can toward the fifty yard line. Then you're in the air in a move that should look familiar to Cordy—your legs go out in a Y in a classic cheerleader jump. Which allows you to knock two of the hole guards to the ground. You were careful not to kick them *that* hard. They should wake up soonish.

When you land, you face off with Cordelia. Kathy goes to stand directly in front of the hole.

"You don't belong here, Buffy," Cordy says.

"That's never stopped me before," you tell her. "I need to get into that hole. You gonna let me?"

Cordelia doesn't answer. She just drops her mouth open . . . *way* open. Her lower jaw falls almost to her chest. And now you see why her face looked strange. Not because of gum or jawbreakers. Cordelia's bones have stretched out. Her jaws are incredibly wide. And while you watch, her teeth lengthen into black fang-type things, jagged and as sharp as knife blades with little barbs all along their sides. She lets out a hiss.

Whoa. What's going on, and why it happened . . . you can figure that out later. Right now you need to get that mouth out of commission. "Sorry, Cordy," you say. Then you swing your leg into a kick.

Cordy grabs you by the ankle, and you're *whomp!* on your back on the ground. You grab some dirt in both hands, arch your back, and spring to your feet. Cordelia and Kathy circle you, snapping their jaws. From the corner of your eye, you see Harmony and the rest of the girl gang running back across the field toward you. You don't have much time.

Whap! Whap! Cordelia and Kathy each get a handful of dirt in the eye. Which allows you to knock their heads together. They crumple to the ground, but you're not worried. You didn't hit them *that* hard. . . .

Harmony has made it back. She doesn't slow down as she approaches you. Which makes your fast kick to her sternum even more powerful. She hits the dirt, and liquid sprays out of her freakishly misshapen mouth. It bubbles and sizzles on the ground.

You catch a flash of motion off to the left. Close. Way too close. You whirl around in time to see a cheer-leader named Holly comin' at ya, with her mouth about a foot away from your shoulder.

You grab the stake from your jacket and jam it between her jaws. *Snap!* The stake breaks. *Thump!* Holly falls to the ground as you kick her legs out from under her. You don't give her time to get back up. You drop down on her chest and give her a little head punch, just enough to knock her out. She should wake up soonish.

Two more people come rushing at you from opposite directions. You're surprised to see that they're not cheerleaders. It's Emily Eiselin from the Young Businesswomen Club and a football player named Billy, or Bubba, or Booboo or something. *Guess it's not just the cheerleaders who have a thing for the hole in the ground,* you think. Emily and the B-boy both spin around to come at you backward, which is unusual enough to make you pay attention. Most people don't attack butt-first.

But then, most people don't have long, pointed stingers where their butts should be. *What the . . .*

You leap back to avoid the stingers, and let Emily and Billy-Bubba sting each other instead of you. They collapse, stuck together at the butt.

As fast as you can, you jump into the hole and climb down the steps that have been carved into the earth. You figure the whole cheerleading squad—and for all you know, the entire Business Club and every varsity sports player in school—will be following you any second. When you reach the bottom of the steps, you find yourself in a long tunnel of dirt. It's narrow, but you can walk upright. Make that *run* upright. You need to figure out what this place is—STAT. Whatever that actually means.

The tunnel widens into a room of earth. Drew

Brody, this not-so-bright guy from your English class, is working on making the wideness more wide with his . . . well, with his big freakazoid clawlike hands. After the mouths and stingers on the guards upstairs, you're beyond being surprised.

"Hey, Drew. Did you see somebody go by here a minute ago?" you ask.

Drew keeps on with the digging. "Anybody want some food in here?" a familiar voice asks. Very familiar. And very, very should-not-be-here.

"Xander?" you exclaim. "What are you doing here?"

"Just checking to see if anybody's hungry," Xander says.

"I am," Drew answers.

"Well, that's what I'm here for." Xander raises his hands to his mouth. His gigantic, amber-colored belly—which, *hello!* is disgusting—begins to heave and ripple. Is there no end to the bizarre physical changes to your classmates? The ripples on Xander's belly grow to waves. Then he pukes. You leap back, expecting Drew to do the same. But Drew just stands there. Xander dumps the green-and-orange and yuck-colored grossness into Drew's hands. And Drew slurps it right down.

You don't need to see any more. In fact, you might need to kneel down before the porcelain goddess if you do. Not that there is anything porcelain down here. Just dirt, dirt, and more dirt. You rush on, trying to make out any fresh footprints.

Which way to go?

You find another staircase and head down, deeper into the earth. You pass more kids from school, working away. No one asks where you're going or what you're doing there. They're digging furiously, as if digging is the new dancing.

You realize that the tunnel you're in is getting wider. And lighter. There is a little runway of light going on made of battery-powered glowing discs. They lead into a swanky lounge with a sofa–love seat combo—

And an Angel-Belakane combo.

They're sitting together on the sofa. She's practically in his lap. Her big dark saucer eyes are staring up at Angel. Her lips are inches away from his. Parted. Ready for big-time smoochies.

With *your* boyfriend.

SLAYER CHOICE:

Do you decide to . . .

\ get out of there? Angel has blown it with you. *If yes, turn to page 158.*

\ stay to see what will happen next? There's clearly something wrong with Angel. He might need your help. *If yes, turn to page 144.*

"You know, Xander? I gotta go," you say. "There's something beyond weird going on. Plus, with the stomach on you and Giles turning into Mr. Romance? The ick factor has gone through the roof."

"Okay," he says. You kinda want to smack him. Does he know any other words? But his sweet Xander face is still as comforting as ever. You have to save him from whatever's taken over his digestive system.

"I'm gonna patrol. Maybe . . ." Maybe what? What are you going to do? Without Giles and Willow, who are the plan makers, you're just a planless Slayer. "I guess I'm gonna, um, just look around and see what I can find. You stay here."

"Okay," Xander says.

"Okay." You give him a pat on the shoulder and take off. You have a feeling that no matter what he said, Xander won't stay in the library until you get back. He's not thinking for himself anymore—that much is obvious.

Outside the school, a few guys from the wrestling team are standing around. They stare at you as you walk by, but none of them move. Weird. It almost looked like they were standing guard or something. But who would want to guard the school?

You file it away for future discussion with . . . well, with someone non-Willow and non-Giles. Eventually you'll find somebody to help you figure this out. And why wait? Angel will be normal, and even if he can't come out patrolling until dark, he can still talk things through with you now. You decide to head over to his apartment.

Five feet later, you're lying on your back with a giant black-gloved fist whizzing at your head. You roll to the side as it smashes down, and leap to your feet, grabbing the large mallet that's fallen next to you as you do. The Sleaninhnam demon stands behind you with a friendly grin on his face and a malicious look in his eyes.

"Where did you come from?" you mutter.

"A hell dimension filled with girls like you being grazed and eaten like cows," he says with a snarl. "Good times."

"I didn't see your little slide appear," you say.

"Maybe you should pay better attention." He swings again. You jump aside. "I want my mallet back," he snarls.

"Let me think about that. No," you say. "What is that thing made of, anyway?"

"Nothing you can break, Slayer," the Sleaninhnam spits. "And when I get it back, I'll use it to break *you*." He swings at you again. You duck the blow and punch him in the gut.

He bends a tiny bit, letting out the slightest "oof." But that's the best you can do. He's strong, he's tall, and he's dangerous. You glance up, spot a low-hanging tree limb, and jump for it. You catch the limb just in time to snap your legs out and kick him in his jolly face. His head snaps back, and his eyes fill with fury.

He gestures with his hand, and the light-side combo appears. He jumps through and disappears into the light.

Good. You have no time for him right now. You have to get to Angel and figure out how to help Xander. And maybe Willow, who's also off her rocker. You take off down the street—and get to the end of the block before the golden slide appears again.

This time the Sleaninhnam comes out fist first, swinging before his black-booted feet even hit the sidewalk. You jump the blow and kick him in the chest on the way. He falls back onto his slide and vanishes.

You run toward Angel. The golden slide shows up again within half a minute. When the Sleaninhnam's feet come through, you grab an ankle and twist. He falls face-first onto the pavement. Immediately he rolls, taking you down with him.

"Give me the mallet, missy," the Sleaninhnam sneers. "No little weakling like you can handle a weapon like mine."

You roll again, ending up on top of him.

You get him in a headlock as he tries to stand. But he grabs your arms and flips you over his head. By the time you're back on your feet, he's swinging at you again. You roll your eyes as you duck—*again*. "Don't you ever get tired of that?" you ask.

"Do you ever get tired of fighting?" he retorts. "It's all you're good for, Slayer."

You run up the back of a car parked along the road and jump him from above, sliding your arm around his neck and holding on. "How do you know who I am if you're from some other dimension?" you ask as you try to strangle him.

His neck is so thick, he doesn't seem to care. "I heard about you through the grapevine," he says. "I guess I must be important to have you all to myself like this."

"Typical demon," you say. "Having delusions of grandeur."

"Well, you're fighting me, aren't you?" He cackles as he digs his big ruddy fingers into your forearm, which is still pressed tight against his throat. "You're not off stopping that ant queen."

You let go of him so suddenly that he falls to the ground. You leap onto his chest and press your knee against his windpipe. "What ant queen?" you ask, but you have a horrible suspicion you already know.

"Belakane. Word on the street says she's about to turn your town into her own personal ant farm." His words come in short gasps as you press on his neck.

"Look, Lucky, I know Ms. Belakane," you say. "And she's no ant."

He gives a gasp of laughter. "Maybe not in front of you," he says. "But once she's finished mating, you'll see more ants than a company picnic."

"Mating? She mates?"

"Mates, lays, hatches, breeds an army, eats the populace," the Sleaninhnam says, and gives another wheezing laugh. "Too bad you won't be around to save them." His fingers reach for your throat. You leap off him just before he reaches you.

"Who is she mating with?"

"How should I know?" He stomps toward you with his giant gold-buckled boots. But you just turn and run.

Ms. Belakane's an ant . . . or a demon . . . or both . . . and she's mating. *And* she's going on a date with Giles any second.

You've got to get to him. *Now.*

SLAYER ACTION:
Turn to page 173.

"Giles!" you yell, racing toward the courtyard outside his apartment. "Giles, you have to stop dating Ms. Belakane! Don't go out with her—"

But you shut up as soon as you see her.

Ms. Belakane in another suit with a pair of stiletto pumps on her feet. Her dark hair slicked back into a French twist. Huge black sunglasses covering her eyes.

And she's smiling.

She leaves Giles's apartment, pulling the door closed behind her. You watch as she *click-clacks* across the courtyard and climbs into the back of a black town car waiting at the curb.

Has she mated with Giles? You can't bear to think about it. You're not even sure what it means for a demon ant queen. But one thing's for sure: It can't be good for Giles. Still, now that you know Belakane's a demon, you have to find out what her big plan is so that you can stop her.

SLAYER ACTION:
Turn to page 174.

The car carrying Belakane pulls away from the curb. You're going to have to follow her the hard way: running.

It's a good thing you've got that Slayer strength, because whoever's driving has no interest in following the speed limit. Or stopping at red lights or stop signs, for that matter. You sprint after the car, hoping she's not headed too far away.

And you're in luck, because the car goes straight to school and drives right out onto the football field.

"Snyder's not gonna like that," you mutter, following the muddy tire tracks through the pristine grass of the field.

The car stops in the middle of the field. You hang back to see what she's going to do. But before Belakane even opens the car door, people begin appearing from holes in the ground. All over the field, kids from school climb from the earth and rush toward the car. Oz and Chris Pearson appear from a hole. Steve Gerli follows Willow out of the main hole. So does Xander. Soon, there's a crowd of people around the car, at least fifty of them.

"What are you doing here, Buffy?"

You turn at the sound of Cordelia's voice. She stands in front of you, backed by Harmony and Emily Eiselin from the Young Businesswomen Club. They're all staring at you through narrowed eyes, and there's something weird about their mouths.

"I'm just out for a walk," you say. The way Cordy's looking at you, you're guessing she's not in the mood to hear the truth about Belakane.

"Walk the other way," she commands. But over her shoulder you see the car door open. Belakane's high-heeled shoes step out. The people surrounding the car all cheer and reach out to touch her.

"I have to talk to Ms. Belakane," you say, pushing past Cordy.

"No." Cordelia opens her mouth, and suddenly you see what was so weird about it. Her bottom jaw drops about six inches straight down, revealing two long, curved, black teeth. Or pincers. You're not really sure they can be called teeth.

Harmony and Emily move in on you too, revealing their own disgusting fang-things. Behind them, you can see Belakane heading into the main hole in the ground, followed by Xander and all the others. You know you should follow her in there and get rid of her. But it's obvious that Cordelia and her cohorts—not to mention your friends—are under some kind of mind control. You'll have to fight Cordy and the other guards to get into the hole, and you'll probably have to fight your own best friends to get to Belakane.

It's not worth it. You still have to make sure Giles is okay. And you'll need help to get into the lair. You do as Cordy says and walk the other way—straight back toward Giles's place.

SLAYER ACTION:
Turn to page 176.

Giles is lying on the living-room rug when you get inside his apartment. One of the end tables lies on the floor next to him.

"Giles!" you cry, rushing over to your Watcher.

He's barely conscious. His eyes looked glazed. You glance around the room. Other than the end table, everything seems normal. "What happened?" you ask him.

"Buffy," he croaks. There's a weird smile on his face.

"Yes, I'm here. Tell me what happened to you."

"Bela . . ."

"Belakane. She did this to you?" you demand.

"She put her hands on my head." Giles's dreamy smile widens. "Her hands were warm. . . ." His eyes close.

"No! Giles, stay with me. Did she—" You break off. You're not sure you can bring yourself to ask him this. "Um, did you guys . . . did you, uh, mate?"

"Her hands were warm. It felt like melting."

You'll take that as a yes. And, for the record, *yuck*. But why is Giles so out of it? "Did she push you down?" you ask. "Why is the end table on the floor? Why are *you* on the floor?"

"I fell," he says. His voice is barely more than a whisper. "I felt so weak."

"Why?"

But Giles is unconscious. You tug him up onto the couch and cover him with a throw. What else should you do? Giles is supposed to tell you what to do in situations like this! Or Willow. She'd know how to handle it. But Willow is off living in a hole with Belakane. So is Xander, and Cordy, and any chance you have of getting help.

"Angel!" You grab the phone and call your boyfriend. When he answers, you're almost ready to cry with relief. "I need help," you say. "Belakane is an ant queen and she mated with Giles and he's passed out and Willow and Xander and Cordelia are all like ant minions or something and I don't know what to do."

"O-kay." Angel sounds like he just woke up. Which he probably did, it being the middle of the afternoon and him being a creature of the night and all. "What do you want me to do?"

"Come to Giles's and help me figure this out."

"I'll get there as soon as I can. It might take a while."

You wince. You'd forgotten the whole can't-go-outside-until-dark complication. "Hurry," you tell him. When you hang up the phone, you're alone again. Giles is still unconscious. You have an ant demon lady on your hands, and she's taken over all your friends. What to do?

You force yourself to think. Normally when a baddie shows up in Sunnydale, Giles tells you all about them: agenda, strengths, weaknesses, likes and dislikes. And when he doesn't know much about them, he and Willow do research. "Research!" you cry. That's what you need! You need to find out as much about Belakane as you can, so you'll know how to kill her. And so you'll know why Giles is lying on the couch, white as a ghost.

You take a closer look at your Watcher. Is he even

breathing? Yes, but his respiration is shallow. His skin is even paler than usual, and that's saying something. He's really sick. Should you take him to a hospital before you do research?

"This is what grown-ups are for," you mutter. How are you supposed to know whether he needs a doctor or not? And then it comes to you like a lightning bolt. You should call Jenny Calendar! She's a grown-up. She's down with the supernatural. And she . . . probably hates Giles right now.

Still, Jenny's your best hope of getting some help. You grab the phone and beg her to come over.

By the time Jenny arrives, Giles has curled into the fetal position. That doesn't stop Jenny from being pissed at him.

"Thank you so much for coming. I totally need your help," you say in a rush.

"You said there was a demon," Jenny replies. "Where is it?"

"It's Ms. Belakane. She's under the football field at school."

Jenny lifts an eyebrow. "And what happened to *him*?" She doesn't even look at Giles.

"Um, I think he mated with her." You glance around the room, trying to avoid eye contact with Jenny. "All I know is that she was planning to mate today, and she came here and . . . uh . . . touched Giles's face . . . and she left all happy and he collapsed." You finally meet Jenny's eyes. "Sorry."

"Why should you be sorry? It was his choice."

"I think maybe Ms. Belakane put the whammy on him," you explain. "Everybody else is working for her. It's like they don't even care that she's an ant."

"Excuse me?"

"Oh! Didn't I tell you? Apparently Belakane is an ant queen. I mean, I've never seen her go all ant-y, but she's an ant queen. And she's building a colony."

Jenny is already scanning Giles's bookshelves, running her finger along the cracked leather spines of the demonology tomes.

"I don't know which book to look in," you say. "I didn't even know where to start."

"I'm thinking Africa," Jenny murmurs, pulling out a huge book. "They have some ant-based legends." Before you know it, she's got you sitting at the kitchen table with about four giant books. You flip through them searching for any mention of antlike demons while Jenny feels Giles's pulse. She doesn't say anything, but you can tell she's worried.

Angel arrives around six thirty, and you still haven't found any ants. He joins in the book-flipping while Jenny makes with the computer research.

"Gotcha!" she finally says. She blows her dark hair up off her forehead in frustration. "I knew that test was a bad idea."

"'Be the Ultimate You!'?" you ask.

"Belakane must have used it to isolate certain personality traits," Jenny says. "Aggression. Nurturing. Organization. People to build her a colony, guard it, and take care of the brood."

"It's true," you say. "Willow helped build this huge underground lair, and Cordelia is patrolling the outside like a Rottweiler."

"Cordelia?" Angel asks skeptically.

"Yeah. And Harmony. And everyone from the debate team, and about half of the Drama Club," you tell him. "It's not pretty."

"Those are the kids who tested strongest for aggression," Jenny says.

"The Peppies," you agree. "It's like they're all brainwashed or something. And some of them are growing ant appendages."

Jenny wrinkles her nose. "Like a normal ant, Belakane can secrete chemicals. Probably a sort of pheromone to help her communicate and control the students she chose for her various jobs. The chemicals must be causing some of the kids to mutate."

"Hey, why does Xander have a huge stomach?" you ask. "He's not aggressive or nurturing or anything. He's just . . . agreeable."

"Huh." Jenny frowns. "Maybe he's a honeypot."

"Well, he *is* being really nice," you say.

"Has he been vomiting?" Jenny asks. "Honeypot ants store food for the others in their nests. Whenever an ant is hungry, the honeypot regurgitates food for them."

"Can we change the subject, please?" Angel says. "What does this ant queen want?"

Jenny reads from the Web page she's found. "A new colony is started by the queen, who mates only once and lays enough eggs to create an entire generation of worker ants."

"Hard to believe that test lady can lay eggs," Angel says.

"Uh-oh," Jenny says, still reading.

"No," you protest. "No uh-ohs."

"This is bad." Jenny shoots a worried look at Giles. "The mating process seems to involve some sort of sucking—"

"I do not want to hear this," you say.

"Sucking of life force," Jenny finishes, shooting you a disapproving look. "The mating leaves the male nearly dead, and he usually does die within a day. His life force has been almost completely drained."

You just stare at her for a moment, trying to wrap your mind around this. "You mean Giles is going to die?" you finally whisper.

"Yes. Unless we do something—fast."

"How can we get his life force back?" Angel asks.

Jenny stares at the computer for a while. "There's no definite answer. But it's likely that if we kill Belakane, the life force she's absorbed will flow back to Rupert."

"Good." You grab your jacket and head for the door. "I'll go kill her."

Angel grabs your arm. "How are you planning to do that?" he asks.

You picture Belakane's lair. A hole in the ground filled with your classmates. Your friends.

"Belakane's colony is heavily guarded," you say

with a groan. "I can't get in without fighting half the kids in school."

"And if Belakane has conditioned them somehow, they may well fight you to the death," Jenny says. "We have to find a way in that doesn't include you killing half the student body."

You stare at the huge mallet you took from the Sleaninhnam demon and gave to Giles for safekeeping. "I bet that leprechaun could jump right inside the lair," you say.

"Leprechaun?" Jenny asks.

"He's a Sleaninhnam demon," Angel tells her. "How is a dimension-hopping psychopath going to help us?"

"I took his favorite toy," you say. "Maybe I can make a deal with him. He jumps me into the lair, I give his mallet back."

"And then you're trapped in a demon's lair with two demons," Angel says.

"Okay. Then I won't give him the mallet until he helps me kill Belakane," you say.

"I have a better idea," Jenny puts in. "If Belakane is using chemical secretions to control the other kids, maybe we can make something similar in the lab. The way regular ants work, all the ants from a colony share the same scent. That's how they recognize one another. If you were with one of their own, or if you smell like one of their own, the guards will let you just walk right in."

"They'll *smell* me?" you ask.

"What if we don't get the chemical right?" Angel asks. "Buffy will be trapped in the middle of an entire nest of ant-controlled guards."

"Well, it's either that or deal with the Sleaninhnam demon," Jenny says. "What's it gonna be?"

SLAYER CHOICE:

Do you decide to . . .

❙ use the pheromone? *If yes, turn to page 184.*

❙ make the deal with the Sleaninhnam demon? *If yes, turn to page 191.*

"**I** don't smell anything," you say.

Angel leans in and nuzzles you. "You stink," he murmurs, kissing his way from your ear down your neck.

"Really?" You take another whiff of your wrist, where Jenny put her laboratory-made demon ant chemicals. "You can smell that?"

He shrugs. "I'm a vampire."

"Don't get cocky." You glance across the football field from your hiding spot under the bleachers. "I guess there's only one way to find out if this stuff works."

You head across the field, Angel following. Both of you act casual when you reach the ring of guards starting at the thirty yard line. "There must be twenty people between here and the entrance," Angel whispers. "I thought you said it was only five or six guards."

"They must have increased security," you say. "I wonder why."

The guards all stare at you. You keep walking toward the fifty yard line, hoping the non-smelly smell will trigger their happy feelings so they let you through. Cordelia steps up and gets right in your face.

"Hey, Cordy," you say.

Her eyes narrow. "Hey, Buffy," she replies. And then she charges straight at Angel. Six other kids follow, all of them attacking at once. You stand, stunned, as he fights them off. Jenny's faux pheromones seem to have worked on you, but apparently they're not vamp-effective.

Angel meets your eyes over the mini-crowd of crazed guards. They've all got their freakishly long, sharp teeth out and they're giving him some competition in the scary fang department. "Keep going," he calls. Then he takes off in the other direction. Cordelia and the others follow him.

You know he'll be okay. You just hope he's not forced to hurt one of them. You keep going toward the entrance to the lair. The other guards there just watch as you climb down into the hole. It's dark, but you've come prepared. You pull out your mini flashlight and pick your way through the dirt hallways until you see it: a bright light up ahead. It's coming from a room dug into the earth at the end of the long hall. You ease along the passageway toward it.

You slow as you reach the room. With your back against the wall, you lean around to peer inside.

The whole place is lit with bright-as-day halogen lamps, which makes it easy to see the decor. It looks as if a Pottery Barn catalog threw up in here. The room is furnished from floor to ceiling, even though the rest of the lair is nothing but dirt.

Belakane lies on the sofa, filing her nails.

"Hi!" you say. "Nice anthill you got here. Too bad I'm gonna have to step on you now."

She jerks her head up, surprised. The nail file falls to the ground. "How did you get in here?"

"Guess I just smell like one of your little drones." You drop into a fighting stance and get ready to attack.

Belakane's dark eyes widen . . . literally. The eyes

grow farther apart as her nose moves forward, turning a dark brown color. Antennae shoot straight up from her head. Her arms lengthen, becoming segmented black legs. Her abdomen extends into a huge, swollen poison sac with a stinger on one end.

You stare at her. The sleek woman in the suit is gone. Belakane is a humongous black ant.

"I guess this means you won't be trading quips with me?" you say.

In response, Belakane lifts her body, tucks her abdomen underneath her, and sprays some kind of funky mist into the air.

"Whoa!" you cry, jumping away from it. "Now *that* I can smell."

Immediately Kathy Boutry shows up in the room. When she sees you, she gives a yell. About five other guards come running. Three of them attack you while the other two rush to Belakane and stand in front of her.

Part of you wants to laugh at the sight of these normal kids protecting a giant, monstrous ant. Belakane's mouth alone is so big, she could bite their heads off with no problem. But she isn't fighting. They are. And you can't kill them.

You start punching. The best you can do is to knock them out for a while so you can get to Belakane.

Bam! You hit Kathy in the jaw. She goes down. "Sorry," you say.

Bam! You hit Emily Eiselin in the jaw. She goes down. "Sorry," you say.

Bam! You hit Matt Lopez from the Model UN Club in the jaw. He goes down. "Sorry," you say.

Bam! You hit Drew Brody from your English class in the jaw. He hits you back.

"Ow!" you cry, shocked.

He punches you again. You catch his hand in the air, and hit him in the jaw with your other hand. He goes down. "Sorry," you say.

The path to Belakane is almost clear. But she shoots some more come-help-me spray into the air, and suddenly there are about ten more people in the room. And all of them are coming after you.

"I don't have time for this," you mutter. You grab a lovely wooden bookcase and yank. It falls to the ground, momentarily cutting you and Belakane off from her rescue team.

She rears up on her back four legs and lunges at you, her huge sharp teeth clacking as she tries to grab you. You spin out of the way and deliver a roundhouse kick to her head. She wobbles a little but manages to spin toward you and bite a hole in your jacket. Her teeth graze the skin of your arm, but you pull away in time.

"That jacket was leather," you complain.

She hits you with a three-foot-long hairy arm, knocking you to the ground. Then she bites again. You roll to the side just in time. You leap to your feet and reach for her while her head is still lowered. You grab an antenna and pull.

Belakane shrieks in pain, and suddenly Greg Zymet

and Rick Muirragi, who are both on the wrestling team, are on top of you. Greg gets you in a headlock. This is bad. They know how to fight—kinda—and you don't have time to be sparring with your classmates when there's a giant ant on the loose and Giles is dying.

You hang on to Greg's arm and use it to pull your weight up and kick Rick with both feet. He goes down. But Belakane steps up. While Greg is holding you, she aims that abdomen-thing at you and gets ready to spray again. You have a feeling the chemical will be a little more deadly this time.

"Looks like a party," says a familiar voice. "If only I had my mallet I could have some fun."

The room is so brightly lit that you didn't notice the white light and golden slide of the Sleaninhnam demon. But there he is, in all his green velvet glory. His blue eyes sparkle at the sight of all the violence in front of him. Belakane backs away from him.

You take advantage of the distraction to flip Greg over your head and get him off you. "I left your mallet at home. Sorry," you tell the Sleaninhnam. "Oh wait, no I'm not."

He swings at you with a black-gloved hand, getting you in the sternum. It hurts. A lot. You swing back, but all you can reach is his stomach. Still, you hit hard. He doubles over with an "oof."

Belakane gets herself back in spraying position. "Poison spray, three o'clock," you tell the Sleaninhnam. He glances at Belakane, and just as you were hoping he would, punches her in the abdomen. She bellows with pain and anger but doesn't spray anything. Good. He's ruined her . . . sprayer.

The Sleaninhnam turns back to you, but Belakane goes after him. She unhinges her jaw and opens her mouth impossibly wide, going for his head. Just as her teeth are about to close on him, he opens a portal. The golden slide appears, and off he goes, vanishing from Belakane's mouth.

Her teeth close on nothing, making an alarming clacking sound.

Kath Lingenfelter from the Young Republicans Club grabs you from behind. You elbow her in the stomach.

Belakane snaps at you, enraged.

The golden slide appears again, and the Sleaninhnam slides back into the room. This time, Belakane is ready for him and she jumps on top of him, crushing him with the weight of her body.

Liz Sullivan from the Future Fashion Designers Club grabs your hair and yanks. "Ow ow *ow*!" you cry. You try to hold her off as you call to the Sleaninhnam demon.

"Hey, Lucky, can you open a portal to a hell dimension? Like a really bad one with no oxygen or something?"

"Of course," he snaps, managing to sound cranky and annoyed even with a giant ant crushing the life out of him.

"Do it," you say. "And I'll push her into it."

"I work alone," he gasps.

"Then you die," you say.

He rolls his eyes. "Fine. But then I'm going to kill you."

SLAYER ACTION:
Turn to page 195.

"**I** vote for the Sleaninhnam demon," you say. "I've got to kill him anyway. Might as well take care of them both at once."

"Fine. How do we get him here?" Angel asks.

"I can do a spell to summon him," Jenny says. She grabs one of Giles's books and leafs through it until she finds what she wants. "Get me a green candle."

"I don't think Giles has—"

"In the linen closet," Jenny interrupts.

You run up to the linen closet. Sure enough, Giles has an array of candles in every color tucked neatly into a wooden box on the bottom shelf. Who knew?

When you get back downstairs, Jenny has made a chalk circle on the coffee table. She puts the green candle in the center, mutters something under her breath— you can't be sure, but it sounds like pig latin—and lights the candle.

Instantly a white light fills the room. The whooshing sound is deafening. And then the golden slide appears. The Sleaninhnam slides in and lands on Giles's welcome mat.

"What?" he growls. Then he spots you. He lunges before his slide is even gone. You kick him in the stomach mid-lunge, and he topples backward.

"Listen up," you say. "I want to make a deal."

He swings at you. You duck under his fist. "Where's my mallet?" he growls.

"You mean this mallet?" Angel hefts it into the air. Which is impressive, because the thing weighs about eighty pounds. The Sleaninhnam leaps for it. You use his momentum against him, jumping onto his back and bringing him down.

"You want the mallet back? Then use your little slide to jump me into Belakane's lair," you say. "I want her dead."

"I want *you* dead," the Sleaninhnam retorts. He gets to his feet, shaking you off like a pesky fly.

"Fine. You can kill me later," you tell him. "But first you have to take me to Belakane. Then open a portal to some kind of bad place."

"A hell dimension," Angel clarifies. "One that will kill her."

"Great. It's a deal. Give me my mallet." The Sleaninhnam makes a grab for it, but Angel jerks it away. He's in full-on vamp mode now, and he looks pretty scary.

"Angel will stay here with your precious mallet," you say. "Then after Belakane is dead, you and I jump back here and you can have the mallet. Not before then."

He sneers at you. But he gestures with his hand and a portal appears, complete with golden slide. "Let's get this over with," he mutters. He grabs your arm and yanks you onto the slide with him. Before you know it, Angel, Jenny, and Giles's whole apartment have vanished. There's nothing but white light and the golden slide.

It's actually kinda fun. For about three-tenths of a second. Then you notice the other end of the slide is shrouded in darkness. You fall off the end into a muddy hallway. Willow and Andrew Wells look at you in surprise, their clawlike hands filthy from digging.

"Wrong place," you tell the Sleaninhnam. "I need to get to Belakane herself. No going through her guards or any of these other people."

He rolls his eyes and opens another portal. The two of you slide through it and land in a different dirt-filled room. This one also has mounds of round, slimy things piled on the floor. Oz and Chris Pearson jump in front of the slimy things when you appear. You've never seen Oz look so mean before. "Stay away," he yells.

You do a quick scan of the big, round room. "No Belakane," you tell the Sleaninhnam. "Can't you demons sense one another's presence or something?"

"We're not *related*," he snaps. He opens another portal. You slide through. This time the end of the slide is surrounded by light. When you get through, you're in a well-lit room filled with new furniture. It can't be the right place.

But the walls, floor, and ceiling are made of dirt.

And Ms. Belakane is lounging on one of the couches.

"This is it!" you cry. "Open a portal to a hell dimension."

Ms. Belakane jumps off the couch. Her dark eyes widen . . . literally. The eyes grow farther apart as her nose moves forward, turning a dark brown color. Antennae shoot straight up from her head. Her arms lengthen, becoming segmented black legs. Her abdomen extends into a huge, swollen poison sac with a stinger on one end.

You stare at her. The sleek woman in the suit is gone. Belakane is a humongous black ant.

"Quick," you tell the Sleaninhnam. "Before she summons her guards."

SLAYER ACTION:
Turn to page 195.

The Sleaninhnam demon gestures with his hand, and the white light appears. A second later the golden slide slams to the ground. If you stare into the light you can see the slide disappearing into darkness. A strange sucking sound comes from the darkness.

"What is that?" you ask.

"A vortex," the Sleaninhnam snarls. "The entire dimension is one big vacuum."

"Cool," you say. "And yikes."

Belakane leaps at you, jaws open wide. As the teeth come closer, you can see that each one is barbed with viciously sharp mini-fangs. You let her get two inches away from you, then shove with all your strength.

Off balance, she stumbles backward. You shove again, getting her giant abdomen onto the end of the golden slide.

The vortex takes it from there. Squealing in anger, her antennae waving about wildly, Belakane is pulled into the portal. The Sleaninhnam laughs . . . until she snaps her teeth one last time, latching on to his leg. He's sucked into the vortex with her.

The last time you see him, Belakane is biting into his head.

And then they're gone. The golden slide vanishes, trapping both of your enemies in the giant vacuum.

They're dead.

SLAYER ACTION:
Turn to page 196.

You're alone in the overdecorated dirt room. You grab your cell phone, wondering if it will work this far below ground.

Nope.

You take off running through the muddy hallways. You have to get to the surface and make sure Giles is okay now.

Kids from school wander around Belakane's lair, looking confused.

"Buffy!" Willow cries as you speed past her.

You dig your heels into the dirt and stop. "Will. Are you back to normal?"

She frowns. "If you mean, am I no longer interested in digging tunnels with my bare hands, then yes."

"Show me your hands," you order her.

She does. They're nice, normal, mud-covered Willow hands. No more claws.

"Hey, do you guys know what happened?" asks Andrew Wells.

"Um . . ." You try to think up a plausible excuse for the whole demon-ant-lair-under-the-football-field situation, but all you can come up with is: "Mind control experiment."

Andrew's ratlike face lights up. "Cool! So that whole test thing was bogus? I knew it!"

"I can't believe he was a Smartie," Willow murmurs.

"I can't believe you were a worker ant," you tell her.

Xander appears around the corner. He's back to his

normal size. "Thank god you guys are here. Do you have any idea what I've been doing?"

"Unfortunately, yes," you tell him.

"I feel sick," Xander says. "How do we get out of this place?"

"Don't you know?" you ask. You turn to Willow. "You built the whole thing. Where's the exit?"

"It's weird," she says. "The whole Belakane thing is starting to feel like a dream or something."

"Ms. Calendar said Belakane squirted you all with some kind of personality-control communications pheromones. Or something."

"Well, the drugs must be wearing off, because all I remember is a haze of disgustingness," Xander says.

"Let's get everyone out before we're all trapped down here," you say. You hand Willow your little flash-light. "You have the best chance of remembering the layout of this place. Lead the way."

"Hey, everybody, follow me!" Willow yells, waving the light around for attention. She heads down the hallway until she finds a staircase, and you all climb up one level. You check your cell. It has a signal here.

You hang back while Willow and Xander keep herding people out of the lair. You dial Giles's number and wait for him to answer.

"Hello?" Jenny says breathlessly.

"Ms. Calendar! Is Giles okay?" you say.

"Buffy?" she asks.

"Yes. Put Giles on."

"He's still unconscious," she tells you. "What happened?"

A chill creeps up your neck. "I killed Belakane. And the leprechaun guy. Why is Giles still sick?"

"I don't know," Jenny says. "But he's barely even breathing anymore. I . . . I think he's dying, Buffy."

You glance up to see Willow at the end of the hallway talking to Oz and Chris Pearson. She doesn't look happy.

"Okay. I'll . . ." You have no idea what to do. "I'll figure something out," you tell Jenny.

You hang up and head over to Willow. "What's going on?"

"I think everybody is out," she says. "But we have a problem."

"Eggs," says Chris. "I think." He looks baffled.

"Hundreds of eggs," Oz agrees. "Maybe a thousand. Maybe two thousand. And they're developing really fast." You look at the two guys. Chris is blinking in confusion. Oz looks less disoriented. Maybe he didn't get zapped with as strong a dose of Ms. Belakane's mind-control juice.

"Chris, why don't you head back up to the surface?" you say. "Oz can tell us about the eggs."

"Okay," Chris says vaguely. "What eggs?"

Willow points with the flashlight. "Stairs. That way." She gives Chris a gentle push.

"Belakane laid eggs as soon as she got into the lair tonight," Oz says. "We didn't know how long it would take for them to turn into ants, but it's going fast. A bunch of them are already moving around."

"The eggs are moving?" Willow sounds horrified.

"I'm guessing no. The eggs develop into larvae or something," you tell her.

"Yeah. They did that." Oz looks grim. "Most of them are about to be ants in ten minutes or so."

"Then let's go kill them," says Cordelia. She and Xander have just come back down the stairs. Angel is with them. You throw yourself into his arms.

"Giles is still dying," you tell him. "It didn't work."

Your friends gasp.

"Mr. Giles?" Oz says. "The librarian?" Now he's starting to look confused.

"Why is he dying?" Willow cries.

"Belakane mated with him by sucking out his life force. We thought killing her would make the life force flow back into Giles," Angel explains.

"The eggs," Willow gasps. "When Belakane laid the eggs, she probably fertilized them with Giles's life force."

"Oh, gross," Cordy mutters.

"Then we have to kill the eggs," you announce.

"Didn't I just say that?" Cordelia asks.

"Where are they?" you ask Oz.

"Down the ramp, at the end of the hall." He points. "Should I come with you guys?"

"No," Xander says quickly. "You get up to the surface. We'll take care of it."

Oz heads off, glancing over his shoulder at you curiously. You don't have time to worry about what he thinks. You run for the ramp.

There's an ant on the way up it.

Not as big as Belakane was. But about a thousand times bigger than a normal ant. "Looks like the eggs aren't eggs anymore," you say.

"The larvae aren't larvae," Willow corrects you. "We have to kill them all if we want to get all of Giles's life force back." She sounds worried.

"Oz said there might be thousands of them," Xander adds. "How are we going to kill that many?"

"Anyone have some bug spray?" you ask. You grab the ant and twist its neck before it has time to react. It drops to the ground, dead. "One down."

"And fifty more approaching," Angel says.

They're approaching *fast*. Running up the ramp toward you like a pack of wild dogs. You attack. So do Angel, Xander, Cordelia, and Willow. "There's too many," you yell over the noise of the battle.

"We need a bomb or something," Xander yells back.

Cordelia rolls her eyes. "Anyone got a bomb?" she calls. "No? Didn't think so." She throws an ant to the ground and jumps on its head with both feet, squashing it. Her face is twisted in a grimace of disgust the whole time.

"Magick," Willow gasps, struggling with an especially nasty ant. You reach over, grab its back two legs, and pull them off. It goes down, and Willow stomps on

it. "We can do a spell," she says. "To reverse the mating, kinda. To make Giles's life force leave the ants and
go back to Giles."

You pull a stake from your jacket and toss it to her.
"Use this. Stab them in the eyes," you suggest. Willow
won't be able to keep killing these things by hand for
very long.

Another ant grabs your arm in its pincers. You turn
your arm with a sudden sharp jerk, twisting the ant
over, then you stab it in the belly with another stake.

"Magick is looking like a good option right about
now," Xander calls.

"Will, can you do a spell like that?" you ask.
Willow's been dabbling with some small magicks lately,
but what she's talking about seems like a major deal.

"No, but Ms. Calendar can," Willow says.

Your heart sinks. "She's at Giles's apartment. I
don't think we have time to wait until she gets here."

Willow bites her lip. "Well, then, I can do it. I'll
call Ms. Calendar and have her tell me how. I'm sure I
can manage it."

"But what if you can't?" you ask. "If the spell goes
wrong, what happens to Giles's life force?"

"I don't know." Willow shrugs. "It could theoreti-
cally just . . . vanish. Or it could stay in the ants. Or it
could go into someone else entirely."

You stare at her. This does not sound like a good
plan.

"I didn't say it wasn't dangerous," she says. "But
what choice do we have?"

"We can keep killing these things one at a time," Angel replies.

You look around. You and your friends have killed ten of the ants already. But there are more ants coming. The entire ramp is covered with them now, and there are probably a thousand more down deeper in the hole. If even one gets away, you lose part of Giles's life force.

But Willow is an inexperienced witch. If her spell goes wrong, you could lose Giles anyway.

What should you do?

SLAYER CHOICE:

Do you decide to . . .

❙ fight all the hatchlings? *If yes, turn to page 203.*

❙ trust Willow to do the spell? *If yes, turn to page 205.*

"It's too risky," you tell Willow. "Just keep fighting."

She nods.

You twist an ant's head, breaking its neck. Then another. Another.

Willow stabs at ant eyes, ant bellies, ant heads.

Xander kicks them, bringing them down. Then Cordelia jumps on them, squashing them with both feet.

Angel grabs their heads by the antennae and yanks, pulling the heads straight from the bodies.

Ant pieces pile up around you. Soon, it's hard to see your friends over all the carnage. But you keep fighting. You retreat down the dirt hallway about ten feet. You can't go too far. You can't risk letting the ants get to the exit. They keep coming. You've lost count of how many you've killed.

"I'm too tired," Willow gasps from five feet away. She's stabbing wildly with the stake, sometimes not even hitting anything.

"Just keep going," you call. "We can do it. They're only ants."

But each ant is as big as a Doberman. And they still keep coming.

Willow stumbles. She falls to the ground. You try to fight your way over to help her, but an ant is already on top of her. It opens its mouth, revealing barbed fangs like Belakane's. You leap on top of it, prying its jaws open wider until they break.

Behind you, Xander screams. You look over your shoulder to see him on the ground. An ant stands on top of him as Cordelia fights to get it off. Two more ants scurry by her while she's busy helping Xander. Angel runs after them, but you can't see what happens. Ten more ants get between you and him. Then twenty.

Willow's still on the ground, but you can't see her face through the ants piling up. They're everywhere, overrunning you and your friends. You've lost the battle. Three ants together hit you behind the knees and you stumble.

The ants keep going, walking right over you, pounding you down onto the dirt. You manage to turn onto your back just as one steps on your chest. It looks at you with its shiny black eyes.

The last thing you see are barbed fangs plunging toward your face.

THE END

"**O**kay. Call Ms. Calendar." You toss your cell phone to Willow. "But hurry."

She runs back down the hallway as she dials to get away from the fight. You turn your attention to the ants. There are more of them every second. You and Angel take on as many as you can, both of you twisting and pulling at the heads. Cordelia and Xander form a sort of assembly line, with Xander knocking the ants to the ground and Cordy jumping up and down on them until they're dead. You've never seen Cordelia fight this way before. All that time as one of Belakane's guards must've been good for her.

"Cordelia!" You throw her your stake. "This will be faster."

"Oh, yuck," she moans as she stabs an ant. "Why do I hang out with you guys?" She stabs another one.

You turn to look for Willow. She suddenly runs back down the hallway and plunges down the stairs that lead to the lower level.

"Where's she going?" Angel asks.

"Dunno." You snap off another ant head. "The ants are coming faster."

"I know," he says grimly.

In a minute, Willow's back. She has an armload of scented candles from Belakane's overdecorated private room. "Does anyone have matches? Or a lighter?" she asks, dumping the candles on the ground.

Xander pulls a metal lighter from his jeans and throws it to her. You all stare at him. "What?" he says. "Chicks dig it when you light their cigarettes."

"Do you even know a single *chick* who smokes?" Cordelia asks.

"Okay, fine. I used to like setting things on fire," Xander replies. "Keep up. We're losing ground to the ants."

Willow climbs over the dead ant bodies to you and grabs a handful of your hair. "Ow," you say, frowning at her.

"Sorry. The spell needs hair or nails from a family member of Giles. You're the closest thing we've got." She yanks out what feels like fifty strands of hair, but only looks like five.

"But I'm not family," you protest. "Won't that screw up the spell?"

"There's no way to know for sure," Willow says. "Giles loves you like family, and you love him. It should work."

"But what if it doesn't?" you call after her. She doesn't answer. She's back on the phone with Jenny Calendar.

"Don't worry, Buff," Xander tells you. "It will work. Willow will make sure we get Giles back."

"Yeah, and besides, we have no choice," Cordy adds. "These ants are totally gonna kick our butts if we have to keep fighting them."

"Thanks for the vote of confidence," you mutter.

"What? I'm just saying we're outnumbered." Cordelia stabs another ant. "You're not *that* much of a superhero."

Willow is busy setting up the spell in the hallway

just beyond your fight. She kneels on the ground and uses her finger to draw a circle in the dirt all around her. She places candles around the circle and lights them.

"Okay, I need a piece of an ant," she calls.

Angel picks up a head and tosses it at her. Willow catches it with a little shriek. She sets it on the ground in front of her and places your hair on top of it. "'Goddess of sky and sea, earth and air, I call on you,'" she says, her voice shaking. Her eyes meet yours. You can see the fear in them.

You clamber over the ants to get to her, stopping right outside the magic circle. "You can do this, Will," you tell her. "I know you can. Get Giles back."

She nods, then clears her throat. Her voice is stronger when she resumes the spell. "'Mother of all, your child's life was taken by force. Release him now. Return him now. Release him now.'" She sets the head and your hair on fire.

You watch, mesmerized, as the strands of hair curl up and disappear into smoke. And then the head explodes into a bright blue flame. The supernatural fire leaps into the air, burning like a pillar all the way up to the roof of the tunnel.

And then it vanishes. The fire is gone. The ant head is gone. Everything is silent.

"Did it work?" Cordy whispers.

Suddenly all the ants collapse. Dead, instantly, every one of them.

"Giles's life force left them," Angel says. "They can't live without it."

"So it worked?" Cordy asks.

You don't answer. You're too busy running for your cell phone. You grab it from Willow and dial Giles.

He answers on the first ring. "Buffy?"

"Giles! Are you okay? Are you alive?" you cry.

"I certainly hope so," he replies.

"Willow saved your life," you tell him. Willow shoots you a big, happy, aw-shucks smile.

"So it would seem," Giles says. "Along with you . . . and Jenny." Ooh. Jenny. The Ms. Belakane situation comes rushing back to you.

"Are you in trouble with Jenny for dating a demon?" you ask him.

He hangs up on you.

"Everything okay?" Angel asks.

"Totally." You give him a kiss. "I'm so glad I have you. How much would it suck to find out you're dating an evil demon?"

"Yeah, poor Giles," Xander agrees. "You never expect your girlfriend to turn into a bug."

"Excuse me? Have you guys noticed? Dead revolting bugs all over the place," Cordelia says. "Let's get out of here."

Willow leads the way out. On the surface, Principal Snyder has already arrived with a bulldozer.

"Summers," he sneers. "I should have known you were behind this. Do you have any idea how much it costs to re-create a state-of-the-art football field like this one?"

He rambles on, but you ignore him. The sun is just rising over the field, all your friends are with you, and Giles will be okay.

It's a great day.

THE END

"We have to go warn Angel!" you exclaim. You rush out the door. Then you have to wait because you do not have the car keys and, even if you did, it wouldn't do any good, because you don't know how to drive. You're the Slayer, and you can't drive. That's so wrong. If you're mature enough to save the world—repeatedly—you're mature enough to drive.

Giles, Willow, and Xander come out, and you manage to get Xander and Willow tucked into the backseat of what they call a "car" in England and what you call a "clown car" in America. Willow is squished against Xander's giant belly, and you feel for her. You get in the front seat. "Drive fast," you order Giles. "And go through all the yellows."

He does. And you get to Angel's—just in time to see Angel driving away. "Follow him!" you yell.

"That was my plan," Giles replies calmly. He turns the car around, and you won't even blink. You are not letting Angel out of your sight. No mating is going on under your watch. No dying, either.

"Do you have more butter?" Xander asks.

"Not in the car, no," Giles answers.

"Does anyone have anything to eat?" Xander asks.

You hand him a tin of Altoids. Willow gives you a reproachful look. "They're sugar-free," you tell her.

"He seems to be heading toward the school," Giles observes.

"Make that toward that skank Ms. Belakane," you mutter as you watch Angel speed toward the Sunnydale High parking lot. He pulls in, squeals to a stop, and leaps out of the car. Yeah, he's eager for some ant lovin'. You remind yourself that he's been chemically altered, just like Xander.

"Stop right here," you tell Giles. You jump out of the car and tear after Angel. You have to get to him before he gets to *her*.

"Angel, wait!" you yell. He doesn't turn around. You put on speed. You catch him just as he reaches the football field and grab his arm with both hands. "Angel, you have to listen to me."

He turns and looks at you. Looks at you but doesn't see you. Doesn't *see* you see you.

"Angel, I know you're here to mate, I mean meet, Ms. Belakane. But she's a demon. You don't feel like she's a demon, because she blasted some chemicals at you. But trust me, she is. All she wants you for is to fertilize some eggs. And it could kill you."

His expression doesn't change. He's not the most emotional guy. But that should have gotten *something* out of him.

No. He turns and keeps walking.

"Fine. Then I'll just have to kill her first," you say, following him.

"I can't let you do that," he says.

You're gonna lose him. You have to try something drastic. Something to shake him out of the Belakane fog. You go up on tiptoe, take his face in your hands, and kiss him.

You feel his hands slide around your neck. Yes. He's responding. This is good.

His hands tighten. Tighten. Too tight. You can't breathe.

You open your eyes. He's looking into your eyes. And he doesn't care that you can't breathe. He wants you to die.

You reach for his throat. Then you remember. Vampires . . . don't . . . need . . . air . . .

Red worms wriggle across your vision. Wriggle across Angel's face. You try to say his name. But you can't speak.

You never would have let an enemy get you in this position. But you love . . .

The red worms explode, turning your whole world red.

Then black.

THE END

"**X**ander. Let's dance," you say. Anything to get away from the freakishness at your table. Even getting in the mosh pit with Cordelia.

"No, thanks," Xander says. "I'm eating." And he sure is. He's on his third hamburger.

"Willow?" you ask.

"Nah." She sounds bored. Oz is standing right next to her, and she sounds bored. What has happened to your friends?

"Oh, I think dancing sounds like fun," Ms. Belakane says. "Oz? Dance?"

"Sure. As long as you don't think it will make you too tired," he says.

"Thanks. I'll be fine." She gets up and heads out onto the floor. The music is some kind of trash metal, not especially danceable for anyone, and absolutely not danceable if you're a grown-up.

"Let's dance!" Willow chirps, running after her.

"No, thanks," Xander says. "I'm eating."

"Didn't Willow just say she didn't want to dance?" you ask Xander.

"Yep."

"But now she's dancing."

"Yep."

You frown as you watch Ms. Belakane, who is now dancing in the middle of a circle of students. They're acting as if she's Julia Roberts or something. And she's not even such a great dancer.

"Look at her!" you say.

Xander does. "She looks great," he says around a mouthful of fries.

Your mouth drops open. Every single person you know has lost his or her mind. And it all seems to be about this one weird Ultimate You! test lady. So what's the deal? Is she really *that* amazing, and you're the only one who doesn't see it? Or are there darker forces at work?

"Xander, didn't you think Ms. Belakane was a freaky totalitarian weirdo earlier today?" you ask.

"Yep." He chugs an entire glass of Coke in one gulp.

"Do you still think that?" you ask.

"Uh . . . no. I think she's cool," he says.

"Why?"

"Because she's cool."

"But what made you change your mind?" you press him.

"My meeting with her after school. She was really cool."

Finally! Talking to Xander isn't usually this much like talking to a five-year-old. He's really acting weird. "You met with her about the test results? What did she say?"

"That I'm a Teddie." He belches. You stare at him. Apparently he's done talking.

"What's a Teddie?" you ask when you can stand it no longer.

"It's an Ultimate You! classification," he says. "Mommies, Teddies, Smarties, and Peppies. There aren't a lot of Teddies. But that's what I am."

Your head hurts. "Are you speaking Swahili?" you ask.

"Mommies have nurturing characters. Smarties are smart. Peppies are aggressive. And Teddies are agreeable," Xander says. "They're the four main personality types. If you know which one you are, you can use that understanding to work to your own individual strength. That's how self-esteem is built!"

The thing is, he's not being sarcastic. That's what you really can't get over. He, Xander Harris, is sitting here telling you all this ridiculous stuff with a straight face. "Is that what Ms. Belakane said to you in the meeting?" you ask.

"Yep. Word for word."

"Why am I not surprised?" you ask. "So let me guess. Cordelia's a Peppie?"

"Yep."

"Of course I am." Cordy bounces over from the dance floor to take a swig of water. "Duh."

When she's gone again, you stare at Xander. He's eating the garnish from the side of the hamburger plate. "You're a Teddie, and that means you're agreeable," you say.

"Yep," he agrees.

"And that's your strongest character trait?"

"Yep."

"What are you supposed to do with that information?" you ask.

"Nothing. Just be the best Xander I can be." He grins. "Hi, Giles!"

You swivel your stool around to see Giles, who's just arrived. He's wearing a normal Giles sweater and normal Giles khakis and his normal Giles glasses. But his face? His face is abnormal Giles. His face is not cringing at the loudness of the music. It is not frowning with disapproval at the rudeness of the students. It is not pinched with confusion at the idea of anyone willingly spending an evening in such a place.

His face is smiling. Glowing, even.

"Hi, kids! What's up?" he says, and you almost choke on your mineral water. He has never once called you "kids" before. He does not use the phrase "what's up?". He sounds positively *American* tonight, and you don't like it one little bit. "Where's Ms. Belakane?"

"She's dancing," you tell him. "And I have to talk to you. We were supposed to have a training session today to talk about that leprechaun. Did you want to do it tomorrow instead?"

"Yes, excellent," Giles says distractedly. "Dancing."

You're speechless. He didn't even correct you when you called the demon a leprechaun. It's official: Giles is 100 percent Out Of It. He scans the mosh pit for Ms. Belakane, and when he spots her, he wades right in to say hello.

You almost grab him to pull him back. You need to talk to him about the Sleaninhnam demon. And, besides, you don't want him to get hurt by the moshers. But

Giles is a big boy. Maybe it's time he learned the perils of the pit.

Shockingly, he survives, even though kids are throwing themselves against him—and one another—the whole time he's in there. It's like he doesn't even notice them, or the music, or anything except Ms. Belakane.

Okay. It's her. She's the weird one. Everyone else is being weird. Not you. You're sure of it now.

When Giles and Ms. Belakane return to the table, they're laughing and talking as if they've known each other for years. His arm is around her waist. They were in a *mosh pit*. The craziness is never ending.

About twenty kids from school crowd around the table as if they can't bear to be farther than ten feet away from Ms. Belakane. "I have to get back up there for the next set," Oz tells Queen Freaky. "I think you should have one more bite of salad before Xander eats it all."

Ms. Belakane giggles and lets Oz feed her a forkful of salad. Giles just smiles as if it's all normal. But it's so, so not.

"See you later." Oz heads toward the stage. You grab Willow's arm.

"Go talk to him," you whisper.

Willow's brow furrows. "Who?"

"Oz! Guitar boy! He's alone right now. Go tell him his band was great before."

Willow glances at Oz. "Nah," she says.

"Will, don't be nervous. He seems really nice."

"I'm not nervous," she replies. But she looks sad.

Ms. Belakane gets up to go to the ladies' room. About fifteen girls offer to go with her, but she shakes her head. "We're here to support Oz and his band," she says. "How would he feel if we all left in the middle of a song?"

"His self-esteem would get lower," Cordelia answers.

"That's right. And I can't have that, now can I?"

Everyone laughs as if Ms. Belakane has just told the world's most hilarious knock-knock joke.

"Don't be long," Giles murmurs. He takes her long, thin hand and kisses it.

Ms. Belakane gives him a slow smile and runs one finger down his cheek. It's like a bad romance movie. And how dare he act all lovey-dovey when he totally likes Jenny Calendar! *She's* supposed to be his new girlfriend, not Crazy Test Lady. You're so relieved when she finally heads for the bathroom.

"Giles, seriously. We need to talk," you say.

"Certainly, Buffy. Go right ahead," he replies.

"No. We need to talk supernatural weirdness that's not appropriate for public consumption," you say quietly. "Can we leave now?"

"Of course not." He seems offended by the idea. "I'm on a date."

He doesn't want to talk supernatural weirdness. You guess there's a first time for everything. You sigh. What now? Ms. Belakane is in the bathroom. It's the first time you've seen her alone all night. Maybe you should go after her and get to the bottom of all this weirdness. But all you really want to do is get out of here. This Ms. Belakane–centered party at the Bronze is no fun at all.

And if you're going to be dealing with the supernatural sans Watcher, you're going to need your sleep. What should you do?

SLAYER CHOICE:

Do you decide to . . .

\ follow Ms. Belakane into the bathroom? *If yes, turn to page 121.*

\ go find Angel? He can't be under Ms. Belakane's spell too. *If yes, turn to page 221.*

You slam out of the ladies' room and run straight for Giles. You've got to get to him before Ms. Belakane does, because . . . whoa.

"Giles," you gasp when you reach his table. "The weirdest thing just happened."

"Wasn't Ms. Belakane in there with you?" he asks, peering over your shoulder. "Is she coming out soon?" He sounds like a pathetic five-year-old whose best friend has left him flat.

"Giles. Focus," you command him. "Ms. Belakane just dropped her lipstick and had a line of ants march it back up to her. Ants. Marching. With lipstick."

"Mm-hmm." Giles keeps staring at the bathroom door.

"For the record, nobody else has ants as helpers when they drop their makeup," you tell him. "Even Cinderella had mice. Who would want ants? What is it with her and the insect world?"

"Mm-hmm. There she is!" Giles leaps out of his seat and rushes over to escort Ms. Belakane back to the table.

You can't take it anymore. She's the weirdest school test lady in history, but nobody seems to care. And Giles obviously didn't hear a word you just said. Or didn't care. Or both.

There's no point in staying here. You grab your bag and head for the door. You need to get to someone sane.

You need to get to Angel.

SLAYER ACTION:
Turn to page 221.

"I mean, ewww, right?" you ask Angel. You kick your heels against the gravestone you're sitting on as you tell him the tale of Giles and She Who Likes Ants. "Would you really want to kiss someone who gets off on bugs?"

"Maybe he's not planning to kiss her," Angel says. He leans in for a kiss of his own, but you're distracted. You've been patrolling for an hour—well, hanging with Angel for half an hour and patrolling for the half hour before that. But you still can't get the image of flirty Giles out of your head.

"How can he do this when he totally likes Miss Calendar?" you ask. "That doesn't sound like Giles, does it?"

Angel runs his hand through his hair. "No." He's frustrated, you can tell. He wants to be making out. And normally you'd want that too. You need to shake off the worry and pay attention to what matters: your gorgeous, sweet, and undead boyfriend. You take his hand and hop down from the gravestone. "Let's take a walk," you suggest.

He strolls along next to you, the two of you picking your way through the cemetery. "You're worried about Giles," Angel says.

"I guess I am," you admit. "He just wasn't acting like himself."

"But you've never seen him when he's dating someone," Angel pointed out. "Maybe this is how he acts."

"All inconsiderate and rude to Jenny Calendar?"

"It's possible," Angel says. "He met this Ms. Belakane,

he was attracted to her, and he acted on it. It's not like he and Ms. Calendar are a couple or anything."

"You're right." He's right. You know he's right. You try to ignore your concern for Giles and turn to look up at your boyfriend. "You wouldn't do that, would you? Meet somebody new and drop me with no warning?"

"No." He stops walking and pulls you into his arms. "Because I'm in love with you. It's a completely different situation." He kisses you, and all your worry melts away. You're lost in the beauty that is Angel.

Light falls across your faces, blindingly bright. You ignore it and keep kissing Angel. But when the odd cracking, snapping, whooshing sound comes, you know you have to check it out. You pull away from Angel and glance over at the light. It's white and pulsing and generally otherworldish. Which means bad. The otherworldish is never good. And the sound keeps coming . . . right up until the giant golden slide appears. As soon as the bottom of the slide hits the ground, the whooshing sound stops. You glance at Angel.

"Is that a . . . playground slide?" he asks.

"For a giant," you reply.

And then, unfortunately, the giant appears. He's eight feet tall, with orangey-red hair and rosy cheeks. He's dressed entirely in a green velvet suit, top hat and everything. He swoops down the golden slide straight toward you, and you get the strangest sense of déjà vu. "Oh, my god, it's the leprechaun from my dream!" you cry.

"There are no such things as leprechauns," Angel replies. "That's a Sleaninhnam demon."

You roll your eyes. "You say tomato—"

"Duck!" Angel snaps. You crouch down just as a humongous black mallet whizzes through the air right where your head was a split second ago. Angel punches the green giant in the chest. The Sleaninhnam demon barely budges.

"The chest?" you ask.

"It's as high as I can reach," Angel retorts. "He's really tall."

The mallet whizzes by again. You both jump out of the way, and you take the opportunity to get a good look at the Sleaninhnam demon. Like the Lucky Charms guy on serious steroids—until he turns his twinkly blue eyes on you. And they are indeed twinkling—with pure hatred. His chubby face twists in a snarl and he swings the giant mallet again.

"What is with you?" you cry. "What do you want?"

The Sleaninhnam snarls again, then gestures with his hand. Another burst of white light fills the air, the whooshing sound starts up again, and another golden slide appears. The demon gives you one last glare, then leaps onto the slide like an overgrown toddler. He slides into the light and vanishes. The light vanishes with him.

"Whoa," you say.

"Sleaninhnams jump through dimensions," Angel tells you.

"Is he coming back?"

The whooshing sound starts up again, and light fills the darkness.

"I'd say that's a yes," Angel says.

"You get him, I'll get the mallet," you tell him. He nods.

This time, you're ready. When the golden slide hits the ground, the demon appears feet first. Angel grabs his ankles and pulls with all his strength.

The Sleaninhnam skids off the slide and lands on his butt, which would be funny if he wasn't so scary-looking with his cheerful suit and his serial killer eyes. You ignore everything else and go straight for the mallet. You grab the wooden handle and tug.

It doesn't move.

Angel jumps on top of the demon and jabs his elbow into the Sleaninhnam's throat. You yank on the mallet again. The Sleaninhnam is fighting to get air—he's not holding on to the weapon that tightly.

"What is this thing made of?" you mutter, pulling as hard as you can. Finally the mallet pops from the demon's hand, and you fall backward with the heavy weapon.

The demon makes a hand gesture, and another slide appears. He brings his knee up and jabs it into Angel's stomach. Angel rolls off him, doubled over. The Sleaninhnam, gasping for air, crawls onto the slide and disappears.

You and Angel stare into the darkness for a minute or so. "Looks like he's sliding somewhere else," Angel says. "I think we're safe."

"He's really strong. And this mallet seems to be made of lead. I can barely lift it."

"Good thing you got it away from him, then," Angel says with a weak smile. "Because *he* can obviously lift it."

"Yeah, and swing it and smash things with it."

Angel shrugs. "They're unpredictable demons. I've only met one; all he wanted to do was beat people up. And then kill them."

You're appalled. "Leprechauns are supposed to be charming and cute and, you know, quirky," you say. "They're all about rainbows and pots of gold and Ireland."

"He's from another dimension. Not Ireland," Angel replies.

You sigh. "I was so busy thinking about Giles that I forgot to be on the lookout for the leprechaun—"

"Sleaninhnam demon."

"Right. I should've killed that thing, and instead I let him get away." You turn toward the cemetery exit. "And I bet Giles won't even care."

SLAYER ACTION:
Turn to page 27.

"**B**uffy!" Willow cries, her green eyes bright with unshed tears. Her voice echoes through your brain. Through your heart.

You have to go stop the Sleaninhnam demon.

"I have to go out for just one sec," you tell Ms. Belakane. "I'll be right back for more of the dancing."

You turn toward the door.

"Buffy," Ms. Belakane calls you, with her low, thrumming voice. You look over your shoulder. She's staring at you with her gorgeous black eyes. "You can't go."

"I have to," you tell her. "Sorry."

Another set of arms rips out of her perfectly tailored little suit jacket. Long, thin, hairy arms.

Those arms whip out and wrap around your throat, strong as barbed wire. You stare at Ms. Belakane. Why is she doing this to you? You love her.

You stare into her eyes, her big saucer eyes. They have divided into fractured sections. You see a little Buffy in each one.

Ms. Belakane's cool new arms squeeze and squeeze. A part of your brain is telling you to punch, to kick, to stake, to claw. But that would hurt her. You can't hurt . . .

The lights in the Bronze flicker. The music spirals down to nothing. You hear Willow scream, but from so far away. Where did she go?

The lights in the Bronze go out.

All the little Buffys in Ms. Belakane's eyes disappear. Everything goes black.

THE END

You want to run across the football field, kick the cover off that hole, dive in, and go after Angel. But what you want isn't always the best idea. In fact, frequently Willow and Giles have better ideas.

"Ants usually have several entrances to the colony," Willow says. "It's for protection, so they always have another way out."

You nod. "Maybe there's a way in from the basement of the school. Let's find it. Fast."

"Fast like bunnies," Willow adds. She gives your arm a squeeze.

Giles pulls out his keys, and you all head to the entrance closest to the library. You pass by the musty, and head down the stairs to the moldy. "I'm afraid the best choice may be to—" Giles nods at a big, round sewer grate. You spot a crowbar propped against the wall that you can use as a . . . crowbar.

You pry open the grate. A not-so-sturdy-looking set of metal stairs leads down into the hole. You head down them and immediately start missing your friends moldy and musty. Because you have just met unholy stinky. Giles and Willow follow you. Then comes Xander. The ladder starts to groan.

"Xander, maybe you could pick up the pace a little," you call.

Clomp, clang. Clomp, clang. That might have been bad advice. Maybe you should have told him to go maple-syrup slow. Because the step under Xander's foot is starting to buckle. It squeals as it breaks in half.

Xander grabs on to the ladder rails. And the ladder

starts to sway. At least he's not too far from the ground. "Just let go!" you call.

He does. You reach for him, and your hands sink deep into his soft, squishy belly as you grab him and stagger back, managing to keep both of you from falling to the floor. "Thanks, Buffy," Xander says. "Are you hungry?"

"No!" you answer. You don't think you have ever been less hungry. You may never be hungry again. What with the stink and the translucent flesh and your hands still feeling like they are in the belly.

Giles leads the way down the sewer tunnel. The walls drip what you hope is water. But the smell makes you not so sure. You try not to think about it. You try to think about . . . no happy thought will come to you down here.

"I think we may have something," Giles says, coming to a stop. You hurry up beside him. He gestures to a section of wall that is earth instead of cement. "This may be a way into the colony."

You all start to dig. Your fingernails weren't designed for this. But eventually you break through the wall of dirt. You feel something that reminds you way too much of Xander's stomach.

"There's something boing-y on the other side," Willow says.

You keep on digging until you've got a hole big enough to crawl through. "Want to do eenie, meenie to see who goes first?" you ask. Then you go first. The ooey-gooey slides across your face. You can't help shuddering as you feel it slide down your body. Then you're out. And you realize that you're surrounded by fifty Xander bellies.

They aren't all attached to Xander. But they are all just as big and squishy and squashy as his. One belongs to Dave from history class. One to Garret Lerner. One to Russ Friend. Basically it's a bunch of the nicest people you know—all swollen to three times their normal size.

"Buffy, is everything all right?" Willow calls through the hole. Her voice is muffled by the tummies.

"Yeah, you guys should come on in," you answer. You decide not to tell them what they'll be coming on in through. You watch their faces as they stand up in the dirt room. Giles—mild disgust, followed by a thorough cleaning of the glasses. Willow—medium disgust, followed by science-girl curiosity. Xander—an agreeable smile, followed by the now-famous words, "Anybody hungry?"

"Anybody want to get out of here?" you ask.

"Lead on," Giles says.

You inch past the honeypot people and out into a narrow earth tunnel that is tall enough for you to walk upright in. "Come on! We've got to find Angel!"

Xander's stomach slurps and sloshes as you race down the tunnel. "Wait!" he cries when the tunnel widens into a room. He stops and heads over to Matt Lopez, who is working to make the room larger by digging out one of the walls—with his humongazoid claw hands.

"Hey, Matt. Want some cookies?" Xander asks.

"Yeah," Matt says.

"One sec." Xander's translucent belly heaves and rolls. Then he pukes into his hands.

"Oh, good god," Giles mutters.

Bile burns your throat and you turn your head away, but not before you see Xander transfer the orange-and-green mess into Matt's hands.

"Come on, we've got to keep moving," you say. Xander will just have to catch up to you when he's done . . . feeding people.

You imagine yourself in one of those plastic-sided ant farms as you and the others travel deeper into the earth. You pass more kids from school, working away. No one asks where you're going or what you're doing there. They're digging furiously, as if digging is the new dancing.

You realize that the tunnel you're in is getting wider. And lighter. There is a little runway of light going on made of battery-powered glowing discs.

Brian Williams from the Debate Club steps in front of you, followed by Jin Park from the Future Home-makers.

"Stop right there," Brian says. His jaw drops down—way down. Practically to his chest. His teeth lengthen into black fangs, complete with little barbs on the sides.

Giles punches him. "Go, Buffy!" he yells. "Get Belakane!"

Willow kicks Jin in the shin.

You hope they'll be okay. You sprint down the

runway of little lights. They lead into a swanky lounge with a sofa–love seat combo—

And an Angel-Belakane combo.

They're sitting together on the sofa. She's practically in his lap. Her big dark saucer eyes are staring up at Angel. Her lips are inches away from his. Parted. Ready for big-time smoochies.

With *your* boyfriend.

SLAYER ACTION:
Turn to page 144.

By the end of the day, you're exhausted. You've been putting out fires for hours—sometimes literally.

"Buff, wait up!"

You stop and turn around at the sound of Xander's voice. It's definitely his voice. You'd know it anywhere.

But the guy walking—*lumbering*—toward you is definitely not Xander. This guy weighs at least three hundred pounds, and it's all in his stomach. Normal Xander legs, normal Xander arms, normal Xander face. And humongous Xander chest and belly.

"Hey." He waves at you with a piece of the cookie he's eating. "What's up?"

You close your mouth, which you suddenly realize is hanging open.

"Cookie?" Xander holds out a bag of mini chocolate chips.

"Xander, have you looked in a mirror lately?" you ask.

"No. Why?"

"Um . . . because you've gained a hundred pounds since lunchtime." You wait for the freak-out.

Xander glances down at his stomach. "I did have a big lunch," he agrees.

That's it? That's his only reaction? Maybe he didn't understand you. "No, Xan, I'm not talking about a bloated stomach. Well, I mean, I *am* talking about a bloated stomach. But not an I-ate-too-much-pasta-and-I-feel-fat stomach. I'm talking about a . . . well, a supernaturally fat stomach."

Xander thinks about that as he downs another cookie. "Nah," he finally says.

Thank all that's holy, Willow appears behind him. She'll back you up in your quest to make Xander freak.

"Will!" you call. "Get over here. Xander is reacting inappropriately."

"I resent that," Xander remarks.

Willow heads over, looking distracted. "Xander reacts to everything inappropriately," she says. "Can I go now?"

"I resent that, too," Xander says mildly. He pulls another bag of cookies from his backpack and rips it open. "Cookies?" He offers the bag around.

Oh, why not. You grab a handful. So does Willow.

"Um, Will?" you say. "Have you noticed Xander's stomach?"

Willow glances at his stomach. "It's big," she says.

"'Big'?" you cry. "It's huge! It's monstrous! It's an evil, supernatural stomach! Nobody gets that fat that fast."

"Whatever." Willow hitches her backpack up on her shoulders. "I really have to go. Ms. Belakane is waiting for me."

Uh-oh. "Ms. Belakane? Why?" you ask.

"Oh, didn't I tell you? I'm helping her with a design project. It's because I'm so smart. Only Smarties are allowed on the design team." Willow says this without an ounce of self-consciousness or irony. She's obviously not herself.

"What are you designing?" you ask.

She shrugs. "You wouldn't understand. Anyway, later." She takes off, munching her cookies.

"Want more?" Xander holds out the bag. As he moves, his shirt rides up over his stomach, and you . . . you can see through it. Not exactly *through* it, actually. More like *into* it. His skin has turned into a sort of amber-colored shell, and inside . . .

Well, it's too disgusting to look at. You turn away.

Xander shakes the cookie bag toward you with a smile.

"No. Xan, come with me," you tell him. "We have to figure out what happened to you."

"Okay." He follows you down the hall and into the library.

"Giles!" you yell. No answer. But the light is on in his little cage of valuable books. You know he's there. "Don't move," you tell Xander.

"Okay," he says.

You run down to Giles's cage and find him flossing his teeth in a mirror stuck to one of the metal slats. "Oh, gross," you cry. This day? She is filled with way too much grossness. "Giles, stop that. We have a situation."

"Can't," he says around the dental floss. "Have a date."

"With Jenny Calendar?" you ask hopefully.

"No—" He pulls a long string through his two front teeth. "Ms. Belakane."

As if you didn't know that. Why is this Belakane person so involved in all things Sunnydale High when she's only been here for a day? Usually it takes at least a week to get popular. And if you're a teacher or administrator or whatever she was, it took . . . well, those people never got popular. "Giles, Xander's become hugely fat and his stomach is see-through and he doesn't care and even Willow doesn't care. Something's going on."

Giles finishes flossing and turns a huge smile on you. "How do I look?" he asks between his clenched teeth.

"Frightening," you tell him. "Now focus. Check out Xander's new physique." You take him by the arm and drag him out of the cage so he can see Xander, who is now eating Cheez Doodles. "See? He's gigantic. He's an NFL player."

"Yes, well, good for him," Giles says. "I really must toddle along now, Buffy, so if there's nothing else . . . ?"

"Toddle along"? Did he actually just say that? You think about it. Is that strange for Giles? You can't be sure.

"Giles, we have to figure out what happened to Xander," you tell him. "Your date can't start this early. It's barely four thirty."

"I'm going to get a haircut first," Giles reports. He sounds like an excited thirteen-year-old girl. "I want to look perfect. And then we're having an early dinner at my place."

It's hopeless. "Fine. Go," you mutter.

"Doodles?" Xander asks, holding out the bag as Giles walks past.

"No, thanks, I just flossed," Giles says. He gives Xander the terrifying smile.

"Okay," Xander replies.

You stare at him as Giles leaves. Xander seems normal in every way. Well, every way except for the humongous stomach with a view. But something is off. Something is non-Xander. "Xan, I think we should set your house on fire," you say.

"Okay," Xander replies. Hmm.

"No, maybe we should hang out with Spike and Drusilla instead," you suggest.

"Okay," Xander says.

"Or how about you go make out with Cordelia?"

"Okay," Xander says again.

That's it! He's agreeing with everything. Xander is usually more the complain-and/or-make-with-the-sarcasm type. Not the agree-with-insane-ideas type. But right now he's all about two things: eating and agreeing.

So what should you do?

SLAYER CHOICE:

Do you decide to . . .

\ ask Xander to tell you what he knows about the current weirdness? *If yes, turn to page 237.*

\ go patrolling and try to figure out the sitch on your own? *If yes, turn to page 168.*

"**H**ey, Xan," you say. "You're pretty fat there."

"Yeah," he agrees.

"Do you know how that happened?"

"Yeah," he says. "I ate a lot. Doodle?"

You take a Cheez Doodle and crunch it. "But Xander, you gained like a ton in a few hours. That's not just from eating. Did something else happen?"

"Yeah. I realized I'm a Teddie," Xander says.

"And that matters . . . why?"

"Because it helped me figure out who I really am." Xander smiles, his teeth covered in orange Cheez Doodle dust.

"Who you really are is an eating machine?" you ask, confused.

"Yeah. Ms. Belakane told me if I kept eating, I could help feed the whole colony," Xander says.

I knew it! you think. "What colony?" you ask.

"Ms. Belakane's colony," he says. "She's building it under the school."

"Oh. That's . . . confusing," you say. "Why is she colonizing Sunnydale High?"

"Because she has to restart her whole civilization here," Xander replies. "Last chance for a Doodle."

"No, thanks." Suddenly you're not very hungry. "So Ms. Belakane is a demon?"

"I guess." Xander pops the last Cheez Doodle into his mouth and shrugs. "She's a queen."

"And now you—and Willow, and Giles—are working for her?"

"I dunno," Xander says. "I'm just supposed to eat."

"But they're all acting weird, and so are you," you tell him.

He just shrugs again. "My job is to eat."

"Xander. Do you know anything about the project Willow is working on?"

"Nope. I just eat."

"Right. Eating. I get that. But you have to help me."

"Okay," Xander says.

"Good. So . . . what kind of demon is she?"

"Um . . . I dunno. I just eat."

You feel like tearing your hair out. On the one hand, this whole ask-Xander-what's-happening tactic is working out better than you could possibly have hoped. But on the other hand, Xander is useless!

"The colony is under the school, right?" you say. "Can you take me there?"

"Okay," Xander says.

Before you know it, you're standing in the middle of the football field. Right on the fifty yard line is a perfectly round hole. Stairs carved into the dirt lead down into darkness. "*This* is the colony?" you ask. It's hard to picture Ms. Belakane with her suit and her boots and her glossy hair climbing down into a hole in the ground.

"Yeah. Come on in," Xander says.

You peer around the football field. It's not really a place where you spend much time. Cordelia watches you from the bleachers. "Hey, isn't that Cordy?" you ask.

Xander glances up. "I guess." He doesn't sound very interested, but you can't imagine what Queen Cordelia is doing out here.

You turn—and see Harmony standing on the twenty yard line. And Kathy Boutry in the end zone. In fact, there are cheerleaders standing all over the field. Just standing and watching you.

"What are they doing here?" you ask.

Xander shrugs. "I just—"

"Eat. You eat. I know." You squint across the field. "Maybe Cordelia's job is just to stand there. Maybe she's like a bouncer or something."

You follow Xander down into the hole. The staircase is shockingly long—it must go an entire story underground. At the bottom, Steve Gerli, a lacrosse player, stands there watching you, just like Cordelia did.

"Hey, Steve," Xander says. "You want a Cheez Doodle?"

"No, thanks," Steve replies.

You frown. Xander finished the Cheez Doodles five minutes ago. He continues down a narrow hallway dug into the dirt. Every so often light streams down from tiny holes bored in the ceiling. The holes must lead back up to the football field. The light is so dim, you can barely see. You follow Xander, feeling more and more confused. What kind of demon makes holes in the ground and fills them with high school students? What does she want?

You peer around Xander. "What's down there?" you ask.

"I'll show you," Xander offers. He leads you down another set of steps into another narrow hallway. Lots of people are down here, digging or just standing around. You and Xander enter a large, round room. This place has only one hole in the ceiling for light. You squint into the darkness, but there's nothing to see. A wide ramp leads up from one side of the room. Otherwise, the place is empty. Oz and three other kids are wandering around the room. Maybe you'll have better luck getting him to explain what's going on.

"Hi, Oz," you say. "What's up?"

"Just waiting for the eggs," he replies cheerfully.

Okay, that wasn't helpful. "Um . . . is that your job?" you ask.

"It will be when the eggs get here," he says.

Maybe another question would be better. "So what's with the ramp?" You peer up the long, shallow hill until it vanishes into the darkness above.

"That's for the eggs," Oz says. "We'll roll them up there during the day to absorb the heat, and then we'll roll them back down here at night. We'll know they're safe down here. Can't be too careful when it comes to eggs."

"Yeeeah," you say. You have no idea what he's talking about. You study him for signs of expanding belly or claw hands. Nothing. "So that's your only job? Rolling eggs?"

"No way. We have to feed them and turn them so they don't mold and help them hatch," one of the other kids says excitedly. "I can't wait!" You look him up and down, suddenly realizing that he's in your American history class. History is first period, so you're usually asleep, but you seem to remember that the teacher made him cry once. Maybe he can help you.

"Chris, right?" you say. "Chris Pearson?"

"Yeah. I'm a Mommie," he tells you, beaming.

"Great. Uh, did you say the eggs were going to hatch?"

"Well, hatch is probably the wrong word. They sort of . . . develop," Chris says.

"Right. First they're eggs, then larvae, then pupae," Oz agrees. "But we take care of all of them. It's an important job."

"Very important." Chris nods so hard, you're afraid his head will fall off. "The most important."

You turn and look for Xander. He's on the other side of the round room, so you call him over. "Xander, you said Ms. Belakane is a queen, right?"

"Right."

You turn back to Chris and Oz. "What happens when the larva thingies grow up?" you ask. Now that you know the eggs will be hatching instead of being scrambled, you're starting to get an idea of what's going on. A *bad* idea. "Do they turn into little Ms. Belakanes?"

"Oh, no. They'll be in their ant form for at least a month," Chris says. "After that, they can change back and forth like Belakane, I guess."

"Ant form?" you repeat. "*Ant* form?"

They all stare at you blankly.

"Xander, she's an *ant* queen?"

He shrugs. "Cheez Doodles, anyone?"

"Yeah. I'm hungry," Chris replies.

And suddenly Xander's stomach is moving. Waves ripple across the globular belly and he begins to retch. You do not want to be watching this. But it happens too fast to look away. Xander pukes up some orange goo, catches it in his hands, and gives it to Chris. Chris shoves it in his mouth—

And you're outta there.

"Does the ramp go all the way to the surface?" you ask Oz, turning your back to the spectacle of Chris eating the not-so-crunchy Doodles.

"No. When the eggs get here, they need to be protected from the outside," he replies. "The ramp brings them up to one level under the surface, but not all the way through."

Great, you think. *No shortcut away from Disgusto-Xander.* "Okay, well, it's been gross," you say. "Gotta go."

"Don't you want to stay and see the eggs?" Chris asks, talking with his mouth full.

You don't. You really don't. "I don't think I have time." You back toward the tunnel you came in from.

"But they'll be here in a few hours," Oz calls after you. "The queen is mating right now. You'd get to see them before almost everybody else."

Mating? Belakane is mating? But she has a date with Giles tonight. . . .

You turn and sprint up the dirt tunnel. You've got to get to Giles. *Now.*

You skid to a stop as Belakane steps into your path. "What did you do to Giles?" you yell.

She reaches out and puts her hand on your arm. "I chose him to be the father of my babies," she says.

What a lucky, lucky man Giles is, you think. *Belakane is awesome. If I were a guy, I'd want to be her baby daddy.*

"And I have a special job for you, too," Belakane continues.

"Really?" Your body floods with warmth. Belakane has a special job for you. That means she thinks you're special, right?

"I'm going to put you in charge of guarding my eggs. Your job is to make sure no one hurts them until they mature and my babies are big enough to rule the planet," Belakane says, giving your arm a little squeeze.

"I would love that," you tell her.

THE END

You decide to take yourself down to Ms. Belakane's office. She's the one who told you how satisfying it'd be to embrace your peppiness. And she was totally right! Hopefully she'll be there so you can tell her.

A whooshing sound, accompanied by a rush of air, makes the back of your shirt ripple. You spin around. And there he is: the Jolly Green Leprechaun. Except he doesn't look jolly. He looks like a cranky baby with his rosy cheeks and big frown. An eight-foot-tall cranky baby.

"You were thinner in my dreams," you tell him.

"Reality adds ten pounds," he snaps.

"Is there any chance we could reschedule?" you ask.

He makes a little peace sign-y gesture with his hand, and another bright light appears. A golden slide whooshes through the light. The demon leaps onto it . . . and he's gone. Huh. Very cooperative of him.

Whoosh! Brilliant light flashes in front of you. And here he comes again. Sliding down another golden beam. This time, you get your eyes off his face and see the massive mallet he has in his hand.

You aren't armed for patrol, because, well, you're in the middle of the school. You have a stake. *A* stake. As in one. You always have one. But that's it.

Mr. Lucky Charms raises the mallet. You drop to the ground as he brings it down and roll left as it smashes into the floor right beside you, cracking the linoleum and smashing the cement underneath.

You pull out your stake and jam it into his hand where it holds the mallet handle. The Sleaninhnam roars in pain and backhands you with his staked hand. You fly across the hallway and slam into a row of lockers. This thing is *strong*.

The Sleaninhnam grunts as he tries to free his mallet from the floor. He's still got your stake in his flesh, but he doesn't seem to mind it. You're defenseless.

Didn't Willow say she had need-to-know info on this guy? You really need to know it right about now. You decide this is one of those situations where it's better to run and live to fight another day—after finding out from Willow how to kill this eight-foot monster.

You race down the hall. You hear the *whoosh*. Bright light right in front of you blinds you for a second, and when you can see again, you realize that the Sleaninhnam demon is coming down his golden beam face-first. The mallet is already raised. It's so huge, it obscures everything else from your vision.

There's no time to react. It's coming down. It's all you can see.

And then everything goes black.

THE END

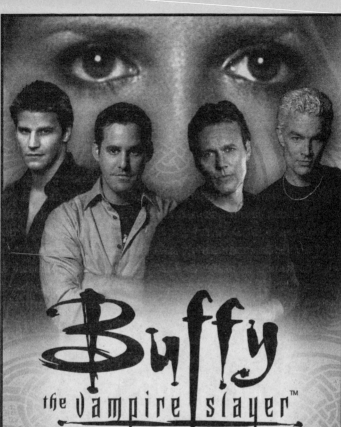